GALLIMAUFRY

COLIN BAKER

Gallimaufry
by Colin Baker

First Published in the UK in February 2012 by Hirst Publishing

Hirst Publishing, Suite 285 Andover House, George Yard, Andover, Hants, SP10 1PB

ISBN 978-1-907959-02-8

Copyright © Colin Baker

The right of Colin Baker to be identified as the author of this work has been asserted by him in accordance with the Copyright, Designs and Patents Act 1988.

All rights reserved. No part of this publication may be reproduced, stored in or introduced into a retrieval system, or transmitted, in any form, or by any means (electronic, mechanical, photocopying, recording or otherwise) without the prior written permission of the publisher. Any person who does any unauthorised act in relation to this publication may be liable to criminal prosecution and civil claims for damages.

Doctor Who and the TARDIS are registered trademarks of the BBC. The final three stories in this book are published with their kind permission.

A CIP catalogue record for this book is available from the British Library.

Cover Design by Robert Hammond

Printed and bound by Berforts Group Ltd

Paper stock used is natural, recyclable and made from wood grown in sustainable forests. The manufacturing processes conform to environmental regulations.

This book is sold subject to the condition that it shall not, by way of trade or otherwise, be lent, re-sold, hired out, or otherwise circulated without the publisher's prior consent in any form of binding or cover other than that in which it is published and without a similar condition including this condition being imposed on the subsequent purchaser.

www.hirstbooks.com

To all teachers who inspire; especially Miss Taverner who was pretty and taught me to read, A.W. (Spike) Martin whose wit first ignited my love of the endless possibilities of the English Language and Ron Smith whose iron will inspired me to learn Greek.

PART 1
This World

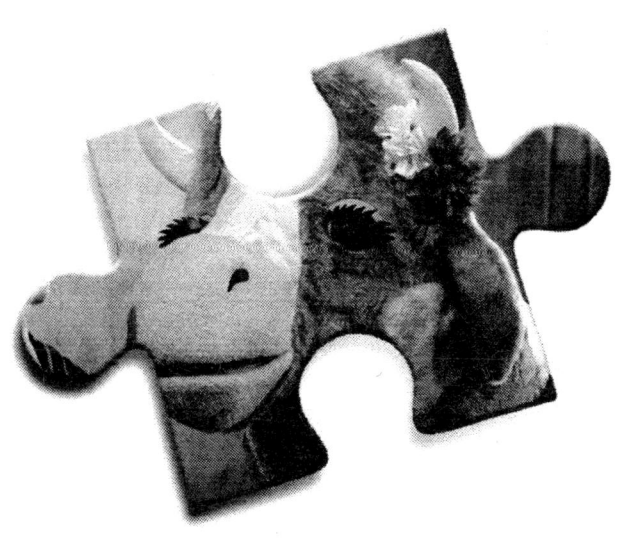

Without Due Care

It had been a good day.

Wayne smirked at the thought of the tightly rolled wad of notes tucked into the inside pocket of the waxed green jacket that he, incorrectly, assumed gave him an air of discreet respectability. In fact, the casual observer was more likely to wonder very briefly where that dreary looking bloke had nicked his Barbour from, before forgetting about him completely. Being instantly forgettable was a very useful characteristic in Wayne's case and interestingly it was one that had also helped to make him what he was. He was determined to 'be someone' whilst that very characteristic of being instantly forgettable enabled him to achieve his ambition repeatedly (i.e. without being apprehended).

The order for a "Land Rover Discovery, green, low mileage and with top spec. trim" had taken him no more than a day to complete. Once he had located it, in the car park behind the Solicitors' office in Castle Street in High Wycombe, it had been the work of seconds for him to be seated in the four-wheel drive symbol of the green-welly brigade and gliding down the M40 towards London. There, he had driven straight to the Steynor brothers' anonymous lock-up under the arches not far from Kings Cross, where a lot of money and very few words were exchanged. The whole operation was conducted in seconds. No one saw the need to check the vehicle out because their brotherly arm was very long and anyone who delivered a sub-standard or (already) dodgy vehicle would very soon have to trouble the NHS for assorted prosthetics. And, it was definitely considered impolite to even think about counting the rubber-band encased notes in front of the burly brothers, whose apparent beaming bonhomie was deceptive and if the payment did turn out to be deficient, what would the

Waynes of this world then do? Complain? Go to their solicitor? So why engage in a pointless ritual dance? In fact, it was considerably cooler and more streetwise, thought Wayne, to toss the wad briefly in the air as if somehow he could, as a result, judge its value by weight alone. The gesture was lost on the Steynor Brothers who were at that very moment both thinking (as twins are prone to do) what a prat he looked in that waxed jacket.

The brothers' overseas clients were even less disposed to display any curiosity about the service history or provenance of the vehicles that were shipped to them – under, as it were, plain wrapper.

Wayne, in common with many of his fellow practitioners and suppliers of good condition second–hand goods to the twins, had turned a hobby into quite a lucrative business. It had only been a few years earlier that he had discovered that he could acquire considerable status in front of his circle of friends by hot–wiring and stealing easy target vehicles. An evening of reckless driving around the housing estates in Oxford and the surrounding countryside had invariably ended with the vehicle being deliberately and comprehensively trashed or, even more frequently, torched, – depending on the effect it would have on either his mates or the sullen, unimpressable teenage girls with whom he had no other effective means of communicating. From the time that he had stolen his first vehicle and experienced the visceral thrill of both the criminality of the act and the reckless speeding that followed it, it had not been long before the simple theft and joyriding alone were insufficient for him. He needed something more. He was a thrill junkie but the thrill needed to be ever more challenging to satisfy him.

He therefore set himself increasingly difficult targets – difficult both from the point of view of the rarity and desirability of the vehicles involved and the attendant risk of discovery and apprehension. Unlike many of his contemporaries, he had never been caught. Being considerably less intelligent than he fondly imagined himself, he had put this down to his consummate skill, rather than the actuality, which was that he had been extraordinarily lucky; a luck that stemmed in part from that very forgettability that forged his personality in the first place. When as a younger boy he had been involved in some stupid vandalism with a bunch of his contemporaries, he was the only one that none of the witnesses identified. Again he imagined that this was because he cut such a fearsome figure that they were afraid of reprisals. The truth, if he had known, would have depressed him unutterably: he was simply forgettable and therefore had been forgotten.

Within the increasingly limited world in which he moved, (frequently far too fast), Wayne's notoriety had come to the attention of the Steynor brothers, who were always on the look-out for a disposable workforce that would be easy to intimidate and therefore completely under their control. They were very good judges of the criminal character and knew exactly which of the many youthful carjackers that came to their attention would never result in a visit from the old bill. Not that that need be a major concern anyway. They had friends everywhere who enjoyed their hospitality in many ways and were always anxious to do a reciprocal favour. That network of friends extended into both the police and the offices of the Director of Public Prosecutions and therefore damage limitation on a minor scale could always be achieved. But they were savvy enough to know that it is always better to let the sleeping giant slumber in case, on waking, its biddability becomes unreliable.

So the Steynors were more than happy to capitalise on Wayne's apparently charmed life and limited intelligence. They were, in fact, able to pay him considerably less than they had to shell out to some of their erstwhile suppliers for goods that they would probably hate to admit were undeniably superior– and moreover they often got next–day delivery. Everyone was happy – except of course the Insurance Companies and their shareholders and the car owners whose premiums soared consequently year upon year. Wayne, however, did not trouble his brain with thoughts of the effect of his depredations upon the rest of the world – a world that did not exist for him in any meaningful way outside the limits of what he himself enjoyed doing and the pursuit of that enjoyment.

So it was that he found himself walking from the station in Oxford to the home he still shared with his mother, the inappropriately named Serena, whose surname was given to her by the husband who had fathered Wayne and then promptly decided that the economic deprivations of the part of eastern Europe that he had only recently left for a better life in England were actually preferable to spending that life with her and Wayne. Serena, however, had not allowed that minor fact to cause her any inconvenience. She had a very busy social life which had resulted in an endless flow of 'uncles' in their shared home just off the Cowley Road. These uncles rarely stayed around long enough to notice Wayne's existence however and neither they nor his mother ever thought to enquire how he could afford his current lifestyle without having a job slightly more productive than "helping a bloke out now and then with a bit of car delivery." He never seemed short of the wherewithal to fund his varied but predictable appetites. He had a fondness for clothes that he believed made him look important and stylish. That fondness was, sadly for him, not translated into actuality. He invariably looked simply 'wrong' – not that anyone noticed, certainly not his 'uncles' or his mother, who had a habit of murmuring, 'You like nice, dear' without even looking up as he left to go out she neither knew nor cared where. He had a vast collection of DVDs of films involving car chases and/or mindless violence. If there were pretty girls in them too that was okay – but it was the cars and the violence he really liked – which eventually, it would turn out, would prove to be rather ironic.

He also owned an air pistol which he used with only occasionally harmful effect (and then by chance) on any small living thing that passed within range of his bedroom window. Wayne had no innate imagination that would lead him to comprehend or pity the suffering of other humans, let alone animals. And his upbringing had done nothing to remedy that deficiency. His only other regular expense was that he had piles of virtually every car magazine ever published (well the glossy ones featuring unattainable dream cars – not the ones telling you how to repair a rusty sill on Ford Cortina).

Perversely, for one so fond of cars, he did not own one himself. By now he could easily have done so, but he simply could not bring himself to pay for something that he could so easily get for nothing. Nor could he retain one of the vehicles that he acquired in this way for his own personal use, without running the very considerable risk of being caught. And for all his limited imagination and education, he was certainly streetwise enough to know what the odds of being apprehended were in most criminal activities and was disinclined to tempt providence by exposing himself to that possibility. The longer he escaped detection, the more doggedly determined he became to continue to do so, and it had to be said that his early luck and subsequent care and attention to detail had rendered him less likely to fall foul of the law than the majority of his criminal contemporaries.

But he felt vulnerable and incomplete when walking. "Pedestrian" for him was a term of abuse – and if a sense of humour had been an attribute of Wayne Thomas Krupinski, he would have found it entirely appropriate to discover that the word "pedestrian" also had the alternative and derogatory meaning of – 'ordinary'.

Ordinary was how he felt when walking. And he most definitely did not like feeling ordinary.

As he plodded along (he saw himself as striding) he fancied that he was cutting quite a dash. Remarkably, he did not adopt the usual accessory of his kind – the predictable sunglasses. This was not because of any presence of good taste in his make-up, but rather because he fancied that his eyes were his best feature. Indeed, in that one respect he may have been correct. They were perhaps his only good feature. They were of a particular piercing blue that is only rarely found in human beings, despite being present in other species, and acquired expensively by many via the use of tinted contact lenses. Had they been owned by someone whose other features complemented their brilliance, they would indeed have been an asset in life. But it was Wayne and for that reason nobody really noticed.

It was definitively irresistible then, when plodding along in this weakened, "pedestrian", state, he saw the gleaming black CAR, standing alone in the lay-by at the edge of the cemetery that ran alongside his shortcut home from the station. For a second, he felt an unexpected tightness in his chest and a quickening of his pulse that he hadn't experienced since that very first Ford Escort only a few short years ago. He had driven it for all of a mile and a half before colliding with a parked car and damaging both sufficiently to ensure that he had to climb out through the passenger window. He and his mate, Shaun had then legged it through the streets, with the blood roaring in their ears and their chests pounding from the exertion, before collapsing behind a wall on the trading estate laughing, whooping and exchanging punches and high fives, whilst indulging in bursts of instant replay along the lines of "Did you see the face of that bloke in the Vauxhall Cavalier when we overtook him on the inside?"

"Yeah, he was well choked! Thought he was going to have a fit!"

"And what about that woman at the traffic lights in the Volvo 245 GLE, when you just missed taking off her front bumper!"

"Yeah – snotty cow – served her right! She should have been looking what she was doin'"

"Man, that was good. We've got to do it again. Soon!"

They did indeed 'do it again soon' but after a while Shaun had attempted to do so on his own, without Wayne who was the dominant partner in that he had both hotwired the cars and then subsequently driven them. Shaun decided that he had to strike out on his own in order to impress a young girl that he fancied on the estate, who had made it perfectly clear that she found him dull and uninteresting. When he crashed the car that they were joy riding in, she lost both her legs and he was sent to prison. Wayne regarded him as a loser and had nothing more to do with him. But whether he acknowledged it or not, it taught Wayne a salutary lesson. Other human beings had no place in the special relationship that he had with the vehicles that he acquired.

Since those early, exciting days therefore, he had adopted a less obviously excited demeanour. He was aware of the concept of cool, even if he did not instinctively own it. But that assumed cool was shattered momentarily by the vision that sat in front of him now, unexpected and impossibly alluring. It only fleetingly passed through his temporarily disabled reasoning process that this could not be happening. This vehicle would not be left here, in this lonely and unlikely place, unattended. In fact, this vehicle could not exist. Nothing that was made by man could be that perfect.

The Steynor brothers wouldn't have touched it; he knew that. It was too particular, too identifiable and could only be owned by someone whose power must surely eclipse even that of the criminal brothers. He couldn't steal it and keep it for himself either – not to use with any regularity anyway. He would have to lock it up forever, away from prying eyes, like those millionaire art collectors, who have secret galleries, housing stolen masterpieces, for their eyes only, to be loved and admired secretly and alone.

None of these thoughts were really formed or completed in his active brain. Thoughts and sensations jostled for his attention and were rendered even less comprehensible by the powerful emotions that overcame all of his usual caution and preparation. He was in a trance of awe, mingled with desire, as he slowly approached the low, sleek limousine. If, many years ago, Mr Rolls and Mr. Royce had collaborated with the Signori Lamborghini and Ferrari and Herr Daimler to hire the creators of the Panther de Ville and the Cadillac to join in a great enterprise and create the quintessential car of everyman's dream, they might, they just might eventually have come up with this magnificent machine. It was so immaculately beautiful that it was impossible to imagine that it was not unique. To have built more than one such gem of engineering and design would have been unthinkable and almost blasphemous. It was impossible to take in its total and harmonious perfection at once. It had to be visually ... sipped. Each square centimetre of the exterior cried out for admiration. The whole was almost too wonderful to assimilate.

As a wine buff savours the bouquet of a rare wine before tentatively rolling the first delicate mouthful around his palate, so Wayne's hand, after involuntarily wiping his palm on front of his chino trousers, delicately made contact with the flawlessly smooth surface of the car. It appeared seamless, the engineering so perfect that feature flowed into feature without the apparent necessity for such prosaic processes as welding or the use of nuts and bolts. Its surface possessed a quality that did not so much repel dust or mud but simply denied its existence or its ability to tarnish its sheen, as its unblemished presence in this distinctly unappetising and muddy backwater testified.

Wayne's hand caressed the contours of the car with a gentleness that might have seemed surprising to anyone who might be tempted to make a superficial judgement based on his public persona. Indeed, he might have been surprised himself had his reaction been predicted in advance of seeing the car. It was as if he seemed intuitively aware that he was, at the same time, both unworthy and the chosen one, though neither of those concepts figured in his everyday thinking. He seized the moment, it was true, with the ardent rapaciousness of a gladiator holding aloft the head of his defeated enemy, but he savoured it also, as if he couldn't bear for the moment of discovery to be over.

To present to Wayne this – even the word "limousine" seemed woefully inadequate – had the effect of disconnecting his involuntary activity lobe from the rest of his brain and give it full control of his body, whilst activating all the pleasure centres at the same time.

Such was the level of his dazed euphoria, bordering almost on a state of automatism, the fact that the driver's door was unlocked and the keys dangling enticingly from the ignition seemed only proper to him and provoked not even the slightest glimmer of doubt or suspicion. He and the car, were, after all, made for each other. It is debatable whether he could have prevented himself from opening the door and getting into the car, if armed police had been guarding it with their weapons primed and pointing directly at him. As he settled, oh so gently, into the soft leather seat, it seemed to adjust itself subtly so that it fitted the contours of his body precisely. The door shut with a firm and almost inaudible 'thunk'. It seemed to him that the car itself sighed with pleasure at the indisputable 'rightness' of his being there. His hand reached out to turn the key.

At this point, Wayne regained sufficient control to slip into the practised procedure of the professional car thief. He glanced swiftly all around and noted that his entry into the car had apparently been unobserved. The cemetery was closed; there were no dog walkers or other pedestrians who might have had the opportunity to notice or, more importantly, remember the improbable sight of Wayne behaving as if he were the owner of this particular car. Even though he thought that he cut quite a dash these days, he was nonetheless sufficiently self-aware to realise that some people might just make a judgement about whether he was the kind of person who might be the owner of this car. But the road was completely deserted. No irate owner bearing down on him, threatening retribution. No children playing. No windows (with or without twitching curtains), overlooking the scene. This seemed only a little odd to him and in fact fitted neatly into his growing theory that he and the car were like a latter day Alexander and Bucephelus, brought together by fate for a glorious purpose. (Not that Wayne had ever heard of the all-conquering Macedonian King or his horse, nor would he have been remotely interested if he had).

But even his relentless pursuit of self-interest and gratification did not prevent him from recognising in himself a sense of profound relief that he had not been obliged to hot wire the car and, in doing so, therefore damage the mechanical perfection within which he now sat.

It was with a thrill of anticipation that he had never experienced before that his hand slowly turned the key. The engine purred into life and was so silent, when idling, that he nearly committed the unforgivable crime of attempting to start an engine that was already running. It was only a gentle squeeze on the accelerator that alerted him to that fact just in time to prevent him from turning the key again. The engine sighed into powerful life, as he selected reverse gear and backed out of the rutted, bare ground where the car had been so carelessly parked. Wayne never made the mistake of driving in a manner that might attract attention, where there was the slightest possibility of his not being able to avoid the indignity and inconvenience of capture and arrest. So he drove the car as unobtrusively as he could, through the streets of low priced, rented housing that stretched to the east from Oxford station.

He could not believe that every head didn't turn as he flowed through the suburban streets like liquid black gold. How could these peasants not appreciate that they were privileged to be in the presence of the most flawless automobile that had ever been created? How could they resist peering to see who could possibly own and drive it? He had initially been grateful for the tinted glass in the car's windows, but gradually started to feel a little irritated by the fact that he could not be seen to be the driver. He was perplexed too by the seeming unawareness of the local population to the miracle that was passing by.

His elation returned, however, when he reached the by-pass and could strike off south and then west letting the beautifully tuned and immensely powerful engine show what it could do. He swept past the John Radcliffe Hospitals up to the roundabout at the Woodstock Road and left the city behind him as he sped off into the rural west of Oxfordshire. He drove for hours. The car had even been sent to him with a full tank.

He swept imperiously down dual carriageways and motorways and had the pleasure of seeing every driver move respectfully aside to let him pass. And why would they not?

One glimpse in the mirror of Wayne in his winged chariot would be enough to engender respect in even the most obdurate outer lane hugger.

He discovered that he could not ask the car to do anything of which it was not capable. Every bend he took just a little bit faster, but the tyres, suspension and shock absorbers never showed the slightest sign of being really put to the test. He realised that in order to really test the car's capabilities he would have to risk more than he was prepared to sacrifice. It wasn't that he was concerned about his own safety; he had the belief in his own immortality that is the province of the unthinking young. No, he did not want to risk damaging the perfection of the car in any way.

Ten years ago he would have done repeated hand–brake turns in the unloved cul-de-sacs of the estates that were bolted on to the eastern perimeter of the erstwhile beautiful city of Oxford. Now he did not want to share his prize. He regained sufficient control of himself to begin to try to address the problem of what he was going to do with the car. He knew he couldn't sell it to the Steynors for onward shipment to the Middle East or Africa. He also knew, however, that to keep the car for himself for any length of time and to be able to use it in such a carefree manner again was impossible. He had already risked more than he had ever done before by so blatantly performing a grand parade through the roads of Oxfordshire and the Cotswolds. He had no idea where he was now, except that it was a country lane in maybe Wiltshire, Gloucestershire or Avon and that it was getting dark.

He put his hand on what he felt should be the light switch. As always seemed to happen with this car, he was right and the headlights sprang out from the front of the car, at the same time as the dials and internal lights filled the cockpit of the car with a subtle luminescence of reds and greens.

He glanced at himself in the rear view mirror, leaning slightly to his left to do so. The instruments' glow highlighted his face in an eerie, almost demonic, way and he flattered himself that it lent him an irresistible, raffish air.

Then happened something for which he was totally unprepared.

As he was practising his version of a cool, mocking smile in the mirror, imagining himself as the master criminal that no man could catch and no woman could resist, his eyes glanced back at the road ahead to see, caught in the white glare of the undipped headlights, a female form standing absolutely still in the centre of the road. The woman was looking directly at him.

She was wearing a loose–fitting, floor length, pure white dress which was billowing in the strong breeze that blew across the road. Her waist length red hair was caught in an eddy of the wind which seemed for a moment to make it stream upwards in a fan of shimmering copper strands. Her head was tilted slightly forwards and downwards, her green eyes riveted to the advancing car for a second that seemed an eternity before she turned, as if distracted, to look at something away to her right. As he hauled violently on the wheel in a frenzied attempt to avoid the inevitable impact with this vision of beauty, he realised that she was no longer there.

The car lurched suddenly to the left as he fought with the steering wheel to keep the car on the narrow country lane. Trees and their exposed, twisted roots and jagged looming braches whirled around him for a few seconds, until he came to a shuddering stop in a fortuitously placed open gateway that led into a flinty ploughed field. The rear of the car came to rest under an overhanging hawthorn hedge, its bonnet glinting and seemingly undamaged in the light of the hunters' moon which dipped in and out of the fast moving clouds.

Of the woman there was not the slightest sign. Had he imagined her? Was his transport of delight such that he had allowed the dappled moonlight, ducking in and out from behind the scudding clouds, to play tricks with his eyes and mind?

Wayne let out a cautious exhalation of relief. Curiously, he was more immediately concerned for the car than he was for himself. His past experiences of manoeuvres of the kind that he had just executed had been accompanied by the thrill of attempting to inflict as much damage to the purloined vehicle as possible, whilst appearing cool and unruffled himself. This time he almost fumbled with the door handle in his rush to get out of the car and check to see if there was any damage. Please no! Please!

Insofar as he could see in the shadows and darkness, there was none. It was quite extraordinary. It was almost as if the car's surface was dirt repellent. Not a speck of the dust storm caused by their waltz through the lane had adhered to the immaculate paintwork. Not a fly on the grill. No haze of pollution. It seemed as serenely immaculate as it had when he first espied it in the road in Oxford all those hours ago.

As he gazed, in mute wonderment, at the car, his spine tingled with the growing certainty that he was being watched. Slowly, he rotated and gazed into the shadows and darkness behind and around him. He completed 360 degrees and he saw … nothing. Heard not a sound, apart from a dog barking in the far distance and the screech of airborne night predators. But he still felt uneasy.

The certain feeling that he was not alone gnawed at the edges of his thought, despite the contrary evidence of his senses. He was distinctly unsettled and of course, the image of that compelling and lovely vision was still in his mind. Was she there? If so, where was she now? Could he have imagined it? Could something that lovely and desirable have been conjured up by mere shadows and tricks of the moonlit night? Surely not. And yet...

Cautiously walking around the car, he made a depressing discovery. After all his frantic imaginings and barely suppressed terror, it could not have been more prosaic, more depressing, more ordinary! Surely not – a flat tyre? This machine, this 'machina ex deis' – could surely not have succumbed to such a devastatingly everyday event as a puncture? Although, even deflated, the front nearside tyre still retained a pristine, undamaged appearance. Whatever had caused the air to escape from the tyre had not marred its surface in any way.

But this was one damaged car from which Wayne simply could not walk away. He knew that there was no alternative. He had to get the car back on the road and spirit it away somewhere. He had already had half completed thoughts about crating it and putting it in store, until he could come up with a means of keeping and using it, if that was ever to be possible. But he had to try. He could not let anyone else take the car away from him; and he could not share it.

But, for now, he had to do something he had never actually done before. He had to change a tyre. He walked slowly around to the boot of the car, still suppressing the continuing nagging feeling that he was not alone, that something or someone was oppressively close and was watching him, even waiting.

He kept checking surreptitiously, (not wishing to look a fool in whose eyes? Perhaps his own.) He forced himself to shake off the nagging uncertainties and fears. He had to be practical. It was perfectly clear, he had now concluded, that the woman had never been there and had been simply the product of his imagination boosted by the euphoria of his union with the car and the effects of the intermittent moonlight streaming through the dense canopy of trees. There were important things to deal with if he were to bring this enterprise to a satisfactory conclusion. And first of all he had to deal with the punctured tyre. He took a deep breath and moved round to the rear of the car.

The boot, he discovered, was as seamless a piece of engineering as the rest of the car. There must have been a gap between its lid and the body work, but in the dark shadow of the overhanging hawthorn it was impossible to see. His hands explored the surface of the boot and he was on the point of thinking that the rear of the car was all one unbroken piece of metal, when suddenly the boot lid hissed upwards tumbling him back into a thicket of blackthorn and nettles, making him curse volubly. The sound of his voice punctured the night air in much the same way as something had clearly punctured the tyre of the car. Bleating with pain and frustration, he struggled to his feet, his hands and neck stinging painfully from the nettles. Putting his hand up to his face, he found a warm, sticky trickle of blood, where a blackthorn spike had skewered his earlobe. He was becoming steadily angrier and more frustrated that this day of a lifetime was being marred by a sudden succession of irritating accidents. Dabbing at the oozing wound with his handkerchief, he reached into the boot with his other hand to find the spare wheel. He had been surprised when the boot lid had opened that no interior light had sprung into life, but his subsequent tumble had driven that from his mind and he had resigned himself to feeling for the spare tyre inside the boot.

Whilst he was groping inside the dark space, he realised he had been holding his breath since the sudden yelp of pain that was followed by an intake of air when the thorn tore his earlobe. He slowly let the air out of his lungs to ease the tension and to help him regain his customary composure..

As he breathed in again, more easily now, his nostrils were violently assailed by a nauseating stench, emanating from the boot of his dream car. At the same instant his probing hand encountered a sticky pulsating wetness within the depths of the dark recess. Before he could adjust to the shock of this discovery, react to these horrific sensations or control his rising gorge, his arm was seized forcefully and swiftly by something within the seething putrefaction. The shock and savagery of the attack was so powerful that his shoulder was dislocated violently as his jerking, writhing body was whipped into the mucilaginous darkness.

His screams of mortal agony and terror were audible only momentarily, as the boot lid sighed shut and the silence of the night was broken only by steadily diminishing wet gurgles from within the sleek exterior of the car – as its digestive juices did their efficient work.

As consciousness slipped very slowly and painfully away from what was left of Wayne Krupinski, he was aware, between the stabs and surges of excruciating torment, of a sighing, melodious crooning in a delicate and irresistible female voice.

There were simultaneous bursts of unendurable agony and equally unendurable pleasure and sensations of inconsolable loss.

A sound of the sea.

A hint of ozone and ... oblivion.

A thin trickle of blood ran across the number plate of the car, leaving not a trace of its passage on the fluorescent yellow background. Wayne had noticed the personalised registration number, when he had so fatally succumbed to the temptation that he had no hope of declining. It had meant nothing to him.

It read C1 RCE.

Circe. The enchantress who had once turned men into beasts in order to consume them one by one at her leisure had evolved over the centuries to exploit the weaknesses of each era and had adapted perfectly to the modern world. After all, mankind had in many cases throughout history saved her the trouble of turning them into beasts, achieving that metamorphosis unaided by her sorcery. She had merely to feast when the mood took her from an ever available and varied bestiary.

She was the perfect predator. She was adaptable, patient and merciless.

Air flowed back into the deflated tyre. The car, now– if that were possible– had acquired an even more lustrous sheen. It moved slowly into the centre of the lay–by.

She waited.

Ill-Gotten Gains

"Thank you for staying with us, Mr McAteer. As a loyal customer you can be assured of a hearty welcome should you decide to return to us in the future. In our experience in the luxury accommodation industry many of our customers love to come back and stay even longer. Perhaps you will do the same ... who knows, eh?"

The words of the warder cut off abruptly as the door swung closed behind Barney McAteer, as he listened with satisfaction to the heavy sound of the bolts being driven home on the massive iron bound double doors behind him. For the first time in twelve years, they were bolts that were locking him out of Callingham Vale Prison. Barney was not a man given to displays of great emotion but he took a deep breath as he surveyed the world outside the narrow confines of his home for the last fourteen years. The air can't have been any different from the air in the exercise yard, but it felt different. Sweeter, fresher, cleaner.

Across the road he saw his younger brother, Jimmy, standing expectantly by the passenger door of his Ford Focus.

"Over here, Barney!" yelled Jimmy excitedly.

Jimmy had always been in awe of his charismatic and popular big brother. He was fifteen when Barney was banged up and he had revelled in the reflected glory of being the younger brother of the mastermind of the Wellington House Safety Deposit Robbery. The break-in over a bank holiday weekend had been meticulously planned and executed. Barney had always favoured the use of brain over brawn and abhorred the use of violence of any kind, let alone that done in the furtherance of crime.

The robbery would never have been connected to Barney without the help and chicanery of an informer. An anonymous tip–off had sent the police to "Cutter" Millington's house in Hampshire to await Barney's arrival, six weeks after the job, with two million pounds worth of bearer bonds, jewellery and cash.

A handgun had been found under the back seat of Barney's car, which, it was subsequently proved, had been used in the Anglo–Australian Bank robbery in Birmingham six months earlier. Despite Barney's vehement and unswerving denial, in the face of all proffered deals and inducements, that he had been involved in that particularly violent robbery, the possession of the gun and his perceived failure to confess and repent that particular crime had weighed heavily against him in court.

"You look great Barn! My God, wait 'til Mum sees you! I suppose it's the gym and all that in there, isn't it? She's always on at me about my weight! But sittin' in a cab all day, what can you expect. It's me meta–whatsits. I can't help it! My Eileen eats twice what I do and she's like a stick insect! Too thin for comfort, if you ask me, eh? Well my comfort anyway! If you know what I mean ! Eh? Oh, sorry, Barn, I mean that's a bit out of order isn't it, with you probably gaspin' for a bit after all these years…"

Jimmy paused in embarrassment at the ever deepening hole he that he seemed hell bent on digging himself into.

"How is Mum?" asked Barney quietly, seemingly unconcerned by his brother's frenetic outburst.

"Oh, you know, Barn, just the same. Always goin' on about somethin'. It's either my weight, or the kids not goin' round to see her, or you not bein' there to deal with all the things that Dad used to do – but she's been countin' the days, Barn. She's been countin' the days till you come back. She can't wait to see you at home again, with a cup of tea in your hand, and she's dead chuffed that you're dossin' down with her for a bit. It must be a pain not bein' able to get back into your own house, what with Sherrie and that bastard of a lawyer in there. You'd have been welcome at my place, you do know that don't you, Barn, it's just Eileen's... well, you know... with the kids and everythin'..."

"Yeah, it's alright Jimmy. Relax. No problem! Let's get going shall we. Mustn't keep Mum waiting after all these years, must we?"

"Right, yeah. Sorry about the car not bein' up to your standard, an' 'at, Barn but it's the best I can do with the cabbin' an all. But I've cleaned it special. Eileen moaned at me. She said I never cleaned it for her and I'm cleaning it for you even though you haven't been cookin' me dinner for the last ten years. Women, eh? Cor, they do go on, don't they?"

Jimmy gave his older brother a conspiratorial wink which he thought indicated that he was now a man of the world like Barney and knew of the strange ways of the opposite sex. Barney smiled indulgently at his younger brother and put his arm round him.

"No problem Jimmy, It's a very nice car – and you shouldn't have cleaned it just for me. Your Eileen's right. She deserves a bit of respect and consideration too. She's the mother of your kids! And I'll bet she's a good cook too, eh?"

Before Jimmy could reply that, in fact, she struggled to provide much more than fried egg on toast and their diet was principally provided by the local chippy, they reached Jimmy's car.

Jimmy opened the door for Barney and he eased himself into the passenger seat and thought about what lay ahead for him now.

The world in which Barney had moved until his arrest had changed over the intervening years. His wife Sherrie, had visited him twice before confessing that during the period leading up to his trial, while he had been on remand, she had been "consoled" by his lawyer Don Grover, who was...

"So kind and gentle that.... well, you know how it is Barney......."

Barney knew only too well. If he had felt any sense of pain or betrayal at the news of his wife's fragility, he did not allow her to see it. He remained externally impassive and seemingly stoical. Inside was a different matter. Both inside prison and inside Barney McAteer.

His erstwhile associates were either themselves long term guests of Her Majesty or had moved into other less risky occupations. There were now a lot of 'chancers' on the manor – druggies and amateurs, who muddied the waters for what he had liked to think of as the pros. He knew that he could not go back to his old ways. In fact he didn't want to. He had changed too and had had plenty of time for reflection and preparation for his re-emergence into society. He acknowledged that his former life involved a large amount of self-deception and that there were no victimless crimes, something that he had allowed himself to believe when he was depriving banks of large amounts of their currency and deposits.

Over the first few days after his release, he allowed life to come to him and took stock, – letting it be widely known that he was 'not interested' in hearing of any tempting offers or schemes. Those closest to him in the old days were curious. He seemed very contained and focused. Despite his avowed intention to forsake his former life and all that went with it, it was almost as if he was biding his time, waiting for something to happen.

And indeed something did happen.

On the tenth evening after Barney's release, Jimmy picked up two fares at The Tanner's Arms and took them to a warehouse by the docks in East London. On arrival, the fares hauled him out of his cab, threw him on the ground, kicked him twice in the stomach and dragged him into the warehouse. He was then hoisted to his knees and found himself gasping for breath in front of a short, stocky man wearing a 'Tony Blair' rubber mask, who whispered hoarsely in his ear—

"Where's Barney stashed the loot?"

"What loot?" began Jimmy, but stopped with an involuntary cry of pain as a boot crashed into his kidneys from behind. His head was pulled viciously backwards by the hair, at the same time as the grotesque masked figure back–handed him across the nose. A warm trickle of blood ran down the back of his throat causing him to gag.

The harsh whisper continued, "Don't mess me about, Jimmy. We know there was another quarter of a million quid's worth of uncut diamonds and negotiable bonds from your brother's Safety Deposit blag – and if you want to walk again, son, you'll tell us where it is!"

The figure raised a hand and beckoned another person who advanced slowly towards him smacking a tyre lever menacingly into his black gloved hand.

"Alright, alright, I'll tell you" he coughed, wincing at the pain his paroxysms caused to almost every part of his body now.

"But if I do tell you, what you gonna do with me afterwards? You're not gonna...?" his voiced tailed off in fear.

"You'll go for a little trip on that boat out there, Jimmy, not exactly 'all mod cons' but you'll have all your limbs intact and you'll be able to look out the porthole – with both eyes! – at the lovely views of the North Sea and by the time you can get to any means of warning your precious brother, it won't matter anymore. Don't flatter yourself, son. You're not important enough to kill! You're just a minor inconvenience. Aren't you the lucky one? So, spill the beans, you pathetic little ponce ... where is it?"

The grip on his hair tightened ominously.

"I don't know exactly..." he began, continuing hastily to avoid the fist which had pulled back rapidly in front of his sweating face, "Barn told me that he hid it in Pete

Strickson's boathouse on the Thames somewhere. But I don't know where the boathouse is or where he hid it, I swear it, please believe me!" he panted, sagging in the arms of the two heavies, who on a nod from 'Tony Blair' dropped him like a sack of potatoes on the floor. The three walked away and went into a huddle for a few moments. Then Jimmy was dragged out of the warehouse and up the gang–plank of a Liberian registered tanker, the grinning Ukrainian crew members of which promptly locked him in a filthy cabin after gratefully accepting the large wad of dollars that was pressed into their eager hands.

Four hours later, Pete Strickson got out of his BMW Convertible and, whistling *Stand by Your Man*, climbed the expensively tiled steps to the front door of his neo–Georgian house in the West London suburb of Ruislip. As he turned the key in the lock, a violent shove in his back sent him sprawling into the hall and skidding across the waxed parquet floor. He crashed into a free–standing dinner gong, which collapsed around his head with brassy reverberations, before spinning around on its edge for an impossibly long time and finally collapsing with a resounding clunk in front of the sprawling Strickson.

As the last echoes died away, Pete stared in disbelief at three dark suits surmounted by the likenesses of Tony Blair, Margaret Thatcher and, most incongruously of all, Mick Jagger. 'Tony Blair' held a wicked looking hunting knife in his right hand.

Pete Strickson had been an "associate" of Barney McAteer's until Pete's indiscretions and love of the high life had led Barney to dispense with his services. One too many failures to lie low after a robbery and show no outward signs of sudden wealth and too many instances of loose tongue syndrome were enough for Barney. Pete was bitter but knew better than to cross Barney while he was at the height of his power within the world that they inhabited.

However, as soon as Barney was banged up and safely out of the way, he had moved in on his territory with the help of some expensive muscle, rather than the force of his own personality. As long as the money flowed freely, he would get his gang of assorted thugs to do his bidding but none of them would have heeded a word of his otherwise. He now ran a direct mail hard porn operation, specialising in some of its nastier aspects.

"Your boat–house. Where is it?" whispered the voice from behind the Tony Blair mask.

"Boat house? What are you talking about. I don't have a boat–house, for God's sake! There's no water within twenty miles of here! Look, I don't know who sent you, but I have protection!. Check if you like, use the phone, for Chrissake! Don't you know who you're dealing with you morons?"

He tailed off as Mick Jagger advanced towards him and kicked him carefully and squarely in the groin, with enough force to make him double over in pain and meet the rising knee with his face. Blood gushed from his broken nose and a muffled voice from behind the Jagger mask complained volubly:

"He's bled all over my shoes, the little git!"

He pulled a net curtain down from the hall window and started dabbing at his light brown Doc Martens.

Strickson slowly realised that he was in the presence of people who either didn't know about his expensive protectors or worse still – simply didn't care! He fought the pain and, still bent double, held a handkerchief to his bleeding nose.

"Wait, please!" he begged "I've got cash upstairs, lots of it. I'll show you. But I swear I don't have a boat house or anything like one. I don't know what you're talking about. You've got to believe me. I'd tell you if I had. Wouldn't I?" He was almost screaming now.

"Get the money!" came the whisper.

He staggered gratefully up the stairs, dripping blood all over the beige Axminster, followed closely by the menacing triumvirate. They watched in silence as he opened the safe behind the Tretchikoff picture of a green lady above his bed and took out £26,000 in banded and packaged high denomination notes.

"Take it... just take it... and go... please!" he sobbed, sniffing and swallowing warm blood between every other word.

Suddenly, the hunting knife smashed down through the back of his hand and pinned it to the mahogany bedside table on which he had been supporting himself. He screamed in agony.

"Now! The boat–house?" came the chilling whisper.

The stolen white van rattled across the wooden bridge and along the grassy track that led down to the single story pre–fabricated chalet beside the Thames. A dilapidated Victorian boat–house adjoined it, under which bobbed a dinghy and a Shetland cabin cruiser.

Blind–folded and gagged, Pete Strickson was bundled up the stairs and into the boat–house. The rubber masks were donned again and the sticky tape ripped unceremoniously from his swollen and puffy face. With his injured hand wrapped in a blood–soaked tea towel, he stared in mute terror at his tormentors. He daren't speak, for fear of provoking another attack. He was under no misapprehension. These men meant business and he realised that his position in the world in which he habitually (and thitherto safely) moved meant nothing to them. His only faint hope for survival, he now feared, was to satisfy them... if he could.

Forty minutes later, the banks of DVD recorders, the makeshift digital studio and the piles of disks, magazines and photographs lay in a smashed and shattered ruin on the floor. The walls, ceiling and floor boards had been torn apart and revealed nothing other than even more sordid examples the products of Strickson's extensive porn empire.

His captors turned silently on their victim to vent their frustration on him, and he knew that whatever was about to happen would be worse, infinitely worse, than what he had endured already. He had no idea what it was they wanted. He would have literally given them anything and everything he had now as the alternative was clearly a slow and painful death. As he was gibbering and begging, while trying ineffectually to scrabble away from the slowly advancing trio, the doors burst inwards and a voice enhanced by a loud hailer proclaimed,

"ARMED POLICE, DROP YOUR WEAPONS!"

Detective Superintendent Ed Rockall sat in Agnes McAteer's sitting room, balancing a cup of tea and slice of Madeira cake on his lap. Agnes had left the room with the stern admonition that her Barney was not be harassed. He had only been out a few days and had been with her practically the whole time. He was a good boy and he always had been. One day everyone would know that there had been a miscarriage of justice. A mother knows her own – and she knew that her Barney was not a wrong 'un.

He had attempted to reassure her that his visit was purely social but her expression made it perfectly clear what she thought of his reassurances and indeed the police in general after the way they had treated her son.

"Well?" challenged Barney, calmly enough, but with the air of a man who wasn't interested in idle chitchat or being messed about. Rockall took the message and responded appropriately.

"We know each other well enough now, Barney, not to beat around the bush. You heard about our nice little collar the other day near Maidenhead, I take it?"

"Yeah, I heard something about that. Well done! Nasty piece of work. Sounds like a good collar."

Barney gave an ironical twist to the congratulation and stared impassively at his former arresting officer.

"Well you know your former associate – Pete Strickson – the one who moved in on some of your territory when you were banged up?

"I know exactly who you mean, Mr. Rockall, though I'm afraid I don't know what you mean by 'my territory'?"

"Anyway, Strickson was running a nasty little porn business down in the Thames Valley and some villains got it into their heads that you had stashed some ill-gotten gains down there. So they gave Strickson a severe taste of inquisitorial GBH, only to find out apparently that they had been led right up the garden path."

"Really? Well, it's is all very fascinating I must say, but I am not quite sure why are you telling me all this?"

"We–ell, first of all it seems that your ex–lawyer, Don Grover, and a heavy called Billy Congleton teamed up with some 'whispering heavy', according to Pete, to tear his place apart to look for some non–existent excess loot from your last job. And secondly, – and this really will amaze you, Barney, – the aforesaid 'whispering heavy' turns out to be your ex–missus Sherrie, in a padded man's suit and a Tony Blair rubber mask!"

There was a slight pause and Barney let out a short laugh.

"You're joking, Mr Rockall! Well I never! My Sherrie? Well, well, well! Who would've thought it. Mind you I'm a bit biased, I confess, seeing as how she gave me the old heave–ho after I was grassed up and framed for something I didn't do. So I am not entirely surprised to hear that she has been a naughty girl. So she's been smacking Pete Strickson about has she? Couldn't happen to two nicer people, eh?"

The Detective Superintendent surveyed him coolly.

36

"Not only that, but Don, being a lawyer, is naturally very well aware of the benefits of co-operation with police when the chips are down and is now being very co-operative indeed. Hard to shut him up, in fact. He now tells us that your adoring Sherrie planted that hand gun in your car to drop you in it for the Anglo-American Bank job. She had got it from Strickson apparently! Are you following all this now? It's complicated!"

Barney nodded impassively.

"Yes I'm following it, thank you, Superintendent. And as a result of what you have just told me, I am waiting to hear your fulsome apology for failing to apprehend the guilty parties originally. But perhaps I am waiting in vain."

"Well, he also informed us that it was your wife Sherrie who tipped us off that we might find you down at 'Cutters' place where we caught you bang to rights with the proceeds of the Wellington House job."

"Who'd have thought it? Well I never! Little Shell! It never occurred to me for one moment that my own wife would grass me up like that. But I suppose her subsequent behaviour when I was convicted should have given me a clue. But it really did never occur to me. The wiles of women eh? Well, I'm gutted Mr Rockall. You can't trust anyone can you? Eh?"

Rockall continued, despite the frustration he felt at the studied calm with which Barney was receiving all his revelations. "Apparently, they recently got wind of the fact that your little brother Jimmy knew something about £250,000 worth of goodies that you had stashed, before you got your collar felt by the serious crime squad. They knocked Jimmy about a bit until he told them you'd hidden it at Strickson's place. But there was no stash! So why would Jimmy say that there was, I wonder? Can you offer us any insight on that little problem, Barney?"

"Wow, that's a tough one Mr. Rockall. I can't think why poor little Jimmy would think that. I hope he's alright – I haven't seen him for a few days. I suppose it's possible that he simply wanted them to stop knocking him about. He's a bright lad, he would have guessed that if an answer was expected then it was a good idea to give one and buy himself some time. That's what I would have done in that case. He probably guessed that they wouldn't take 'No' for an answer. And he's had a quiet life has Jimmy. He's a good lad. He's not used to dealing with people like that!" suggested Barney, helpfully.

"Turned out quite well for you hasn't it?"

"How do you mean, Mr Rockall? I don't quite understand... Turned out well in what way?"

Superintendent Rockall took out his inhaler and took a puff at it as he stared at Barney looking for a crack in that oh so controlled demeanour. He couldn't help but admire the man and felt a grudging respect for what he believed Barney had so cleverly orchestrated.

"Well... where should I begin? You've got rid of all the people who framed you and got you sent away for a fourteen stretch and you've got your Sherrie out of your house for a good many years. Probably even longer than the term you've just served."

Barney looked at Rockall thoughtfully and slowly nodded as if discovering a great truth for the first time.

"You're right, Mr. Rockall. You know, I never thought of that. I see what you mean. Yes, it has turned rather well for me hasn't it?"

"What I want to know is who started this rumour about the hidden loot and who tipped us off about what was going on?"

"So do I, Mr Rockall. So do I. If you find out, you will let me know, won't you? I probably owe them a drink, don't you think?"

"I know what I think, Mr. McAteer. I think we've got some very nasty people under lock and key and I think that you would be very well advised to do everything within your power to ensure that the terms of your parole are strictly observed, don't you?"

Barney nodded carefully again, as if weighing up the significance of what Rockall had said. Then it seemed as if a sudden thought interrupted his thought processes.

"Am I entitled to any compensation for my wrongful conviction, Mr Rockall? I don't expect an apology, of course, but I could do with a bob or two. What do you think?"

"I'm the wrong person to ask. I think you should take advice from your lawyer about that, Barney. Oh sorry. I forgot. He's going to be in prison for quite a while too. It looks like you'll need to find a new lawyer now, won't you? Let's hope, whoever it is, that they have your interests more at heart than the last one, eh? And if you want my advice, I'd keep him away from any new lady friends you may have in the future."

He looked Barney straight in the eyes and nodded with a half smile, which was met with a bland look of innocence as the superintendent turned and left the room, just as Agnes McAteer returned to top up their tea.

"Everything all right, Barney?" she asked anxiously.

"Couldn't be better, Mum. Couldn't be better," he replied, giving her one of those smiles that had always made her feel special. She gave him a hug. Her big boy was back.

Later that evening Jimmy called Barney from Gdansk.

"How did it go, Barn. Did I do well?"

"You did *very* well, Jimmy. I'm proud of you! But I'm a bit cross with you, bruv, you should have told them straight away. I told you not to get hurt!"

"If I'd coughed too soon they might have sussed, Barney. They would expect me to be hard, wouldn't they? After all, they do know I'm Barney McAteer's brother!"

"Of course they do, Jimmy, I'd forgotten that. Silly of me. I'm sorry! Are you alright then?"

"Yeah, I'm fine. The blokes on the boat were actually really great. They looked after me a treat and we had a right laugh even though their English wasn't too good. I'll tell you all about it when I get back. What about things your end? Can't wait to hear all about it. You're brilliant, Barn, you really are. Only one thing though... I couldn't help thinking: Wouldn't it be great, if there really was some stuff stashed away somewhere? That would really be a result."

"Yeah, Jimmy, it would, wouldn't it? But dream on Jimmy, dream on. Now hurry back home. Mum's anxious about you. I'll pick you up at the airport and we'll bring a curry back here, eh?"

He put the phone down and walked across to the dresser where his mother kept her collection of Toby Jugs. On the top shelf there was one with a policeman's helmet and truncheon. He took it down and blew the dust off it and reached inside.

He pulled out a safety deposit key and stared at it thoughtfully before putting it back with a smile.

Poison Pen

Chief Superintendent Barksfield surveyed the heap of incoming mail with disfavour. He had enjoyed being a 'hands–on copper' for well over a quarter of a century and had only accepted his latest promotion with reluctance, principally in order to gain the increase in salary that went with it. His two sons were fast approaching their last years at the local Grammar School and were both showing gratifying signs of acquiring grades good enough to gain entry to the University of their choice. But, despite their undoubted ability and commendable hard work, it was probable that they were unlikely to achieve the very highest standard that might gain them the scholarships or bursaries that could in turn ease the resultant financial burden on Jim and his wife, Teresa, a primary school–teacher.

The net result was that Jim Barksfield was doing what he had always vowed he would never do. He was now a pen–pusher, a form filler and successor to the man who had so regularly irritated him over the previous years with his seemingly dogged obsession with procedure, P.R. and budgets. Now, and for the foreseeable future, he was himself to be that same irritant to others and he found the role uncomfortable.

He sat in the bare surroundings of the Chief Super's office surveying the patches on the wall where had hung his predecessor's collection of photographs that celebrated the sporting glories of his younger days. The recently retired Chief Superintendent O'Shaughnessy had been a very successful middleweight boxer in his youth, although his sporting activity in later years had been limited to the odd trophy won with the County's Police Golf Society. Jim Barksfield had not yet decided what might suitably replace the empty spaces on the wall. He had supposed that he ought to make the place reflect his personality but at the moment felt diffident about doing so. He was very much a family man and would probably import a few photographs that might serve to remind him of why he was there instead of out in the real world interacting directly with the public to whom he still retained an unwavering commitment, despite having on many occasions witnessed some of the worst aspects of human behaviour in the course of his investigations. At the moment the glaring patches, that so startlingly attested to the length of time that had passed since those walls had been painted, served as a salutary reminder of the newness of his position and the act that he had to follow.

He had always shared an office before, as the chief constable favoured the open plan arrangement that was very much in vogue at the time. Now, suddenly he was alone, behind a closed door and felt strangely unmotivated in the absence of the ever present friendly banter and the cut and thrust with his fellow officers.

But there was work to be done.

Today's batch of incoming mail included the usual lengthy directives on Policy and amended Codes of Practice, complaints from the public, advice on media briefings and invitations to speak at Rotary Clubs, W.I.s and other community groups and, in addition, the routine inter–departmental memos.

He slit the envelopes with the letter opener presented to him by his erstwhile colleagues on his recent elevation in rank. It was engraved with the legend *'The pen is mightier than the truncheon'*.

"If only that were true..." he thought ruefully, as he read the inscription again.

The contents of the envelopes were consigned to the stack of coloured trays, which he had mentally labelled "urgent", "sometime" and "never", although he would never explain to others the significance of his colour coding system of filing.

It was a system that he had inherited from his predecessor and was the one piece of procedure that Jim had gratefully accepted from Brendan O'Shaughnessy.

"James old son" he had drawled in his deceptively beguiling Kerry accent, "The best piece of advice I can give you, as I leave this room for ever, is not to waste your time on stuff that needn't ever be done. Concentrate three quarters of your time on the things that really can't wait, and allow most of the rest of your time for the stuff that shouldn't be put off for too long. I know you probably think that I am a pedantic, nit-picking old dinosaur," he had added brushing away Jim's half-hearted attempt to protest, "but I tell you – that way, you'll keep your head above water, and more importantly the Chief Constable off your back! And always allow a little bit of time to smell the roses, James me boy!"

He had then had opened a drawer, taken out a half empty bottle of Jamesons' whiskey and without so much as a backward glance had sauntered out of the office that he had so ably dominated for nigh on twenty years.

Jim scanned a letter from Jephcott and Mallow, Solicitors, Notaries Public and Commissioners for Oaths, to see which tray would prove to be appropriate in this case.

He read:

"Dear Supt. Barksfield". Clearly his recent promotion hadn't penetrated the solid bastions of the town's oldest firm of solicitors, he thought.

"We enclose herewith a sealed letter, which forms part of the effects of our late client Marcus Webb and which the trustees of the estate have directed should be passed on to 'The chief investigating officer in the case of the murder, in 1991, of the late Jeffery Marsh'. We understand from our enquiries that you are that officer. In the event that you agree with us that, given the particulars of the aforesaid instruction to the trustees of Marcus Webb's estate, you are the appropriate recipient of this sealed letter, please acknowledge safe receipt of the contents on the attached form of receipt and sign the indemnity attached. It should be made absolutely clear at this point that we have no knowledge of and can therefore accept no responsibility, legal, moral or actual for the content... etc. etc."

Jim Barksfield raised his eyebrows in interest. He had spent many long sleepless nights wrestling with the still unsolved murder of Jeffery Marsh, theatre critic, celebrity and self–styled wit. His investigations had been painstakingly thorough, lengthy and ultimately inconclusive. There were so many possible suspects, each of whom might have had very good reason for wishing to hasten the demise of this most unpleasant and vitriolic man, that it was only Jim's innate professionalism that was affronted by his failure to bring a guilty party to trial for his death. There was no great press of people urging that the case be kept open, nor did anyone even think of castigating Jim in any way for his team's failure to find anything that might lead to a successful prosecution.

Jeffery Marsh was not greatly loved. He had been prepared to sacrifice friendship, other people's careers, personal relationships and colleagues' respect in the interest of maintaining his status as the infamous 'Poison Pen' of Fleet Street. He revelled in, rather than felt affronted by, the soubriquet that more sensitive souls might perhaps have found uncomfortable. Countless actors and directors had been heard to wish him a slow and painful death, when they found their careers and livelihoods threatened by reviews that brimmed with personal attacks, withering scorn and – most damaging of all – the neat phrase, chosen for its pithy mordant wit rather than accuracy and which lingered longer in the reader's memory for that very reason.

Marsh had happily free-loaded off the great and the good, who regularly entertained him lavishly in the forlorn hope that they might thereby escape, even temporarily, being the butt of his poisoned barbs. However, when the moment arrived when he perceived his advantage as being greater in their demolition than in benefitting from their erstwhile generosity to him, he had no compunction in, as one wag put it, "...writing off the hands that fed him".

Few, therefore, mourned when he had been found dead at his home on the outskirts of the Hampshire village of Lower Pelling. The cause of his death was strychnine poisoning. It had been a classic closed room scenario and whilst motives abounded, opportunities and evidence appeared non-existent. The only clues had been a series of anonymous letters, threatening his imminent execution, which had been cut and pasted from Marsh's own words printed in assorted newspaper reviews and books. Marsh had taken these to the police who had been unable to trace the sender. They had all been posted at different London mainline stations and the most painstaking forensic investigation had yielded no clues. Marsh had taken the threats seriously enough to spend a large sum of money fortifying "Narcissus Cottage" to the extent that the emergency services had been unable to gain entry in time to save his life after he had pressed the panic button he had recently had installed when overtaken by the first fatal convulsion.

No trace of strychnine had been found in the house – other than the concentration in the arched and contorted corpse. The pathologist's report had concluded that the poison had been taken over a period of time and the last had been some hours after he last ate or drank. The case had started out as a mystery and remained an impenetrable enigma all these years later.

In a final gesture of contempt for the rest of humanity, Marsh had left his not inconsiderable estate to a publisher with whom he had had a long-standing feud, with the proviso that he should, "within three years publish a series of anthologies of my theatrical critiques and essays". To his credit, the publisher allowed the estate to lapse to the State under the intestacy laws rather than yield to the insufferable megalomaniac in death.

Jim Barksfield broke the wax seal on the back of the envelope, opened it and removed the audio-cassette within. He could not resist playing it immediately and set off in search of a means of doing so.

Half an hour later, having borrowed a colleague's less up-to-date cassette player, he settled down in his office and pressed 'Play'.

"Inspector Barksfield. I hope that by the time you are listening to this tape this you will either be Chief Constable — or have retired. To be honest, I suppose that by saying that, I am simply wishing myself a long life, rather than expressing a genuine concern for your career advancement.

However, I am not sure whether I owe you a debt of gratitude or whether I should congratulate myself on a job well done. Shall we say the latter, as I am sure you are a highly competent officer? I am, as you will have now perhaps realised, referring to the death of the unspeakable and loathsome Jeffery Marsh. During the investigation of his murder, one of your sergeants came to talk to my late sister, not knowing of her death as a result of an overdose of tranquillizers some months earlier. He was very kind and apologised for troubling me so soon after my loss.

Somewhat surprisingly, it transpired that the sergeant and I shared a love of gardening, in particular the propagation of hybrid roses. We remained in close contact for some years and derived considerable mutual benefit from our common passion, which it seems he felt unable to share with his colleagues. I am unsure whether he saw that as a deficiency within himself or he was suggesting that his fellow officers were not as susceptible to the many benefits to be derived from the gentle art of horticulture. He clearly did not fit the accepted stereotype of a police officer, so I suspect the latter. Anyway, I digress.

He told me that he was visiting a number of people who might have had cause to wish harm to Jeffery Marsh. My late sister had been an actress, whose career had never recovered from a savage review of her performance as Cleopatra at the London Shakespeare Festival some years earlier. It actually destroyed her confidence, rather than restricted the offers of work, which were still, gratifyingly, many. Despite the perceived surface bitchery, the theatrical profession can rally round in the face of a common enemy and it did so in my dear, lovely Constance's case. But, alas, she could never quite expunge the memory of being referred to by Marsh as (and I quote): "a stilted and posturing performer, who has for far too long strained the audience's willing suspension of disgust. How a post–menopausal woman, with the figure of a sculpture rejected by Epstein and a voice not so much projected as hurled into the face of an unsuspecting audience like so much rancid offal, could have the gall to accept the role of Cleopatra in the first place defeats this reviewer. Age has most certainly withered her and the Egyptian Queen's "infinite variety" seemed extremely stale (to the point of decay) to this reviewer. My sympathies to the asp, which was the most animated participant in the final scene, despite the sagging frugality of its last meal."

As usual, he had offered the sensation junkies and the harpies who feed on the humiliation of others their daily sacrificial lamb. And my darling Constance was never able to shake off the viciousness of the attack. The coroner's verdict of 'Accidental Death' was a direct result of the last act of kindness of a sympathetic doctor to a gentle and broken woman. By that I do not mean that any member of the medical profession assisted her to kill herself. It was rather that he was sufficiently human to attest that the fact that she had taken too many pain killers was more likely to have been the result of an error rather than a deliberate act.

My greatest pain was that none of the many people who loved her were able to succeed in helping her to sustain her self–belief in the face of this vile and heartless attack. Despite my best efforts as her loving brother and the support of her friends, she remembered only those savage words and could not believe that another human being could have such an opinion of her, were there not at least a grain of truth in what they wrote.

Along with her many friends and fans I stood beside her grave and threw a handful of earth down upon her coffin, along with a bloom from her favourite rose in our garden – one that could have been named after her – the beautiful, dark pink 'Sweet Unique'. As I walked from that sombre graveyard on that inappropriately bright, sunny afternoon, I resolved to kill the man who had, in effect, murdered my sister. I would like to say that I wished to do so in order to spare others the agony and shame that Marsh had heaped so casually upon Constance, as if she were of no consequence at all and could therefore be crushed like a mosquito.

But I suspect that revenge was my true motive and through this letter read by you 'post mortem' I am prepared to accept that that was the case without shame or regret. However as soon as I embraced my mission, I realised that there was no reason to sacrifice myself in order to achieve my objective.

Various plans foundered at an early stage of their conception because of the distinct likelihood of my being caught. I started to read detective fiction avidly in the hope that Colin Dexter or Dorothy L Sayers could point me in the right direction. But, of course, in their books even the most inventive of killers is brought to justice by the genius of the detective or a small flaw in their plan. Weeks passed by as I avidly researched various means of ending a life, (I forbear to say 'human life' in this case, as in my eyes Marsh did not qualify for such a description.)

But it was finally an article in a TV listings magazine about Marsh's daily life that neatly solved my problem. He had allowed some sycophantic journalist to trot along behind him for a week while he expatiated tediously upon the wonderfulness that was Jeffery Marsh. There were few details of his tedious life that were not shared with the subservient hack and us.

He was, it transpired, a man of strict routine and was obviously more than slightly susceptible to flattery. Every time the journalist praised him (in ways that most of us would find uncomfortably excessive) Marsh preened himself and shared more of the detail of his self–obsessed life. I discovered that he had no secretary and indeed no administrative help of any kind – who, indeed, could bear to work regularly for such a loathsome specimen? He answered all incoming mail personally, each day in the late afternoon. He only answered fan mail (Yes – I was amazed to discover that he actually received fan mail!) if the sender sent a stamped, self–addressed envelope. But in that event, he confided to the reporter, "How could I refuse to engage with my public? After all without them, there would be no–one to read my humble offerings." Anyone who knew Marsh knew that what he really meant to say was "Without the compliant swine out there – there would be no–one to appreciate the pearls I cast before them."

Having completed his afternoon's correspondence, Marsh would then walk down to the village post box with his dog (a miniature poodle, naturally) in time to catch the 4:45 post. I suddenly knew my opportunity had come. I had already been sending him anonymous letters threatening his imminent demise posted in different locations in the London area. It was gratifying to learn later, via the gutter press that he had fed and fed off so diligently in life, that he had taken the threats seriously enough to seek expert security advice and barricade himself into his home. It was also heartening, but hardly surprising, to learn (when one or two of the letters were published in the newspapers after his death in the hope that someone might identify the handwriting), that others had also felt the need to instil the fear of death into the poisonous little man.

My letters however were all written on a computer and printed out on an old printer, long since jettisoned. But the news that he had fortified his country retreat was very heartening, as my one fear had been that the untimely use of a stomach pump might save his execrable life and thwart my desire for revenge. I then changed my literary tack, as well as the paper, fonts and style of my writing. I started to write the most fulsome letters of praise to him; it was hard to do initially but I started to warm to my difficult task.

I always took care to enclose a self-addressed, stamped envelope 'for the favour of his reply.' And each envelope that he so thoughtfully licked and returned to me was... 'special', of which more later. Each review he wrote prompted me to a new level of praise for his sharpness of intellect and impeccable artistic courage. In fact, I even began to believe that I had some ability myself in the field of literary endeavour.

As I had dared to hope, given the revelations I had read in the newspaper, he replied every time I wrote to him and smugly accepted all my flattery, with only the occasional bout of self–deprecatory posturing. He truly was a thoroughly loathsome man. My final letter enclosed a large colour photograph of Marsh, which I asked him to kindly sign and return. I had previously purloined some strychnine from the garden shed of a happily careless friend, (before it had been made illegal for those purposes), who had long forgotten that he had ever acquired it to deal with a mole that had been disfiguring the billiard table smoothness of his much loved lawn. Being rather fond of Moldy Warp and his shy friends, I like to think that I made much better use of the small amount of poison that I had taken than my neighbour would.

I had mixed the strychnine (an amazingly small amount it seems is sufficient to achieve its fatal effect) with a flavoured soluble gum which I coated carefully on the flaps that ran along the edges of the assorted envelopes that I had enclosed 'for favour of return.' They all came back to me and were destroyed instantly. Having read up on my subject avidly in the public library (without drawing attention to myself by taking out any of the books on loan) I had formulated a plan of administering gradually increasing amounts of the poison over a period of weeks. I calculated (happily correctly) that my final dose would accomplish the lancing of the boil that had festered in my life for so long. I sent Marsh a large colour picture of himself that I knew he favoured as a flattering likeness and requested that he signed and returned it to me.

I had coated the long side of a specially made A3 envelope with my mixture of gum and strychnine in a quantity that I was convinced would deliver the coup de grace. This particular concoction I had flavoured with edible essence of rose as my researches had informed me that he had a penchant for rose flavoured Turkish delight and it seemed appropriate to me given my sister's passion for roses. The envelope was returned to me the day after his death, containing the photograph dedicated to me by name and bearing the suffix 'a rare man of sound judgement and impeccable taste.' I was rather taken by the realisation that for once in his worthless vile life – albeit right at the end of it – he was absolutely right. Having achieved my objective, I was able to dispose of the only evidence of my execution of the vermin that was Jeffery Marsh by the simple expedient of popping the crucial envelope on the drawing room fire beside which my sister and I used to sit on many winter evenings in happier days.

And I had achieved that objective without ever, to my knowledge, having the unpleasant experience of encountering my victim in the flesh. Not only that, but the victim had obligingly returned to me the evidence while the poison was actually working its cleansing effect. Obviously, I have never been able to claim credit for what I truly believe was the finest act of my otherwise uneventful life, which has been a source of some slight chagrin over the years.

I must add, for the sake of clarity, that I have never for a second regretted what I did. Somehow though, I need to let knowledge of my deed live after me, even if only in your mind, Mr. Barksfield. Whether you choose to noise my guilt abroad is a matter for you alone, I suppose. Part of me would still like to protect my sister from the public stigma that is so inhumanely attached to a suicide, but another part of me earnestly desires the exposure of her vile murderer for what he was. I will leave that last decision to you.

As for me, the fact that you are now reading this means that the bubble reputation troubles me now not a jot. As Cleopatra's handmaiden said, 'The bright day is done and we are for the dark.'"

Jim Barksfield listened to the static hiss of the tape for a few seconds until the cassette player turned itself off. He stood up and walked across his office to look out of the window. A moment later he sat down, tucked the cassette into his jacket pocket and lifted the first letter from the purple "Urgent" Tray.

A Likely Story

"I never cease to be amazed at the brazen effrontery of criminals who appear before this bench and, in the face of overwhelming evidence to the contrary, attempt to excuse their gross and flagrant lack of respect for the rule of law by asking us to believe stories that a five year old would deride as incredible. Today we have been asked by you, Mr Farley, to accept that your presence in your unfortunate victim's dining room at two o'clock in the morning was the result of a telephone call, from a third party (whom you cannot produce), requesting that you take part in a 'challenge for a popular television programme' that does not exist.

The fact that you have presented before this court this insultingly unlikely tale as evidence of a lack of criminal intent on your part convinces us not of your innocence but merely of the fact that you are foolish as well as felonious. We would normally be disposed to accept arguments from your learned counsel that a first offence of this kind should be dealt with by a probation order or community service. However, in the light of your unrepentant stance, as evidenced by your singularly childish, offensive and persistent denials of guilt, I am convinced that a custodial sentence is more appropriate in this case. You will go to prison for six months. Take him down please, officers."

As the hapless Farley was led down the steps to the cells to await transportation to Wormwood Scrubs, Leslie Ormerod Stacker sat back and looked around the court room with that expression on his face which many others in the past had found so infuriating. It indicated smug satisfaction in a job well done and, at the same time, challenged any liberal do-gooders to defy his God-given moral right to deliver a this particular short sharp shock to the dejected Farley.

The two female magistrates that sat either side of him looked intently at their papers. Mrs. Baggot had suggested that she had found his excuse mildly entertaining in an otherwise dreary procession of wrong–doers. But she was a Liberal Democrat, thought Leslie dismissively, consigning her along with Greens, Hippies and even the Salvation Army to that soft underbelly of society – the insipid and "well meaning", who were obstacles to the restoration of decency, order and discipline in world that was too frequently deficient in any of those desirable qualities.

Thankfully, noted Stacker, Mrs. Deakin–Brown was more visibly impressed by the unassailable logic of his arguments. He was blithely unaware that her anxiety to jump the lengthy queue in the waiting list to join the golf club of which Leslie was the Honorary President played a more significant part in her wholehearted support of his implacable position than did her belief in the validity of that position. The fact that Mr. Baggot's dahlias had beaten Mr. Deakin–Brown's floral offering to second place in the South Surrey Flower and Produce Show did not, of course, affect her decision to support Leslie Stacker.

After a stunned pause, as he was descending the steps, Farley turned and erupted: "But it's the truth, I tell you, they said if I did it, we could win an all-expenses paid holiday with the kids in Torremolinos, you miserable..."

Mercifully for his chances of avoiding a further period of incarceration for contempt of court, his intended description of Leslie Stacker was cut short by the heavy clang as the door to the subterranean cells was thrown open against the wall below the court, heralding a trip to somewhere demonstrably less beguiling than Torremolinos. Although, the arresting officer was heard to murmur words to the effect that he had been to Torremolinos with his family the previous summer and knew where he would rather be going right now. The food and company, he added, were likely to be considerably better in the nick, not to mention the view! And Spanish telly was terrible: all in ruddy Spanish! Honestly, these crims – they didn't know when they were well off! And at least the wife's sister wouldn't be giving <u>him</u> constant grief about not helping the wife with the kids, and it being <u>her</u> holiday too! Nobody deemed it advisable to point out to him that at least he had the option of popping down to the Bar a Gogo for a swift Pina Colada or a pint of Stella when domestic bliss became unendurable. And they were right to forbear from doing so because Sergeant Ellison was a man who didn't care much for people who pointed things out to him.

Some hours later, Bill Farley was contemplating the cell which he was to call home for the next few months. His cell mate was relishing the opportunity to share with his dazed companion the love of animals and taxidermy which had led him to purloin people's cherished pets in order to immortalise them on the shelves that housed his extensive collection. The other prisoners had long since lost patience with "Paxo" Gudge. His tendency to elaborate on the finer points of his hobby just as the beef stew was being ladled on to their plates was not a characteristic that had endeared him to them.

"Paxo" had been caught, literally red–handed. It was rumoured that the police dog accompanying the officer who arrested him had not yet recovered from the emotional trauma of greeting another German Shepherd in the traditional manner and finding itself sniffing formaldehyde rather than the expected exciting new variation of an intimate canine aroma.

At the same time, five hundred miles away, as Bill was digesting information about the delicacy of touch demanded by the formidable challenge of a deceased Chihuahua, Leslie Stacker, magistrate, director of education and chairman of the town twinning committee, was settling into the slightly more salubrious accommodation offered by the Claymore Hotel in Inverness. But it would have been no consolation to the incarcerated Bill to know that Leslie, too, was not overjoyed by the situation he had found himself in. He was reluctantly attending a two day seminar for lay magistrates that offered insights on, amongst other things, sentencing policy. He had noticed with considerable chagrin that one of the speakers was to address them on "The role played by inappropriate custodial sentencing in the creation of a recidivist criminal sub–class."

He had allowed himself the luxury of a rare half smile when it had occurred to him that he would prefer to deliver a lecture himself, on the subject of "The incidence of pick–pockets re–offending after amputation of the hand".
Leslie was proud of his sense of humour. "Just my little joke" was one of his favourite sayings, along with "I was beaten regularly when I was at boarding school. Didn't do *me* any harm!"

He had arrived in Inverness to find that the Convention Hotel had been overbooked and unfortunately, as a later arrival, he would have to be accommodated elsewhere. His displeasure was intensified when he arrived some three quarters of a mile away at the alternative hotel to which he had been despatched (rather brusquely, he thought) by the lady from eastern Europe who was manning the reception desk at the hotel he had booked. He discovered that he was now being accommodated in a modern, impersonal multi–storey monster, which was hosting a Fantasy/Science Fiction Convention during the period that he would be there.

The foyer was seething with semi–clad girls in greasy make–up and enthusiastic young men in ill-fitting Star Trek uniforms. Not that Leslie knew the source of the inspiration for the costumes. He took a certain pride in regularly announcing to anyone within earshot that he 'never watched television', in much the same way that evangelical teetotallers might declare that they 'never allowed alcohol to pass their lips' in a tone of voice that implied that beer and wine were the work of Satan's evil hordes.

Leslie did not believe that television had contributed anything useful to society that could not have been achieved by healthy exercise and regular visits to the public lending library. And once in the library he himself considered the non–fiction section less fraught with risk than forays into the dark recesses of the fiction shelves, where heaven knows what depravity might lurk within the pages that were the product of imaginative minds.

Leslie negotiated the hotel's corridors that were teeming with alien life, all desperate to be seen and admired by their peers and therefore constantly moving with pretended purpose around the hotel. He finally closed the door on room 7143 with a sigh of relief.

His luggage was due to follow him from his original Convention Hotel, along with the bags of the other handful of delegates who had been similarly obliged to transfer to The Claymore. He availed himself of the services of the tea making equipment and, perched on the end of his bed, he ate the small packet of rich tea biscuits and the chocolate mint that had been placed upon his pillow. He had not cared to see the juxtaposition of the potentially messy chocolate and the crisp white pillow and found a trifle irksome the prospect of leaving it there until later in the day when he might forget its existence and wake in the middle of the night smeared in chocolate. He resolved that small dilemma by eating it immediately after he had consumed the complimentary biscuits.

Still perched on the end of his bed, as there were no chairs in his room, he then read through the paperwork for the convention several times until he had thoroughly acquainted himself with the minutiae of the scheduled events.

Finally, having waited as long as he could bear for his suitcase and the hanging bag for his dress suit to arrive, Leslie picked up the telephone and contacted the reception desk to complain. He was told that it appeared that it had been mistakenly placed on the wrong pile of luggage by the porter and had unfortunately then been conveyed along with the archdeacon of Wells to the station, whence it had accompanied him on his railway journey to Edinburgh. The archdeacon was clearly a man of probity, 'being a man of the cloth', and would doubtless realise the error on arriving at his destination and arrange for its prompt return. Sadly they had no forwarding address for the archdeacon and would have to wait for him to contact the hotel. They would then arrange for delivery of the luggage to his room, hopefully before breakfast the following day and was there anything they could do to make his stay more comfortable in the meantime? Could they perhaps provide him with a complimentary bottle of their house wine from the restaurant?

Leslie curtly dismissed their offer and decided to retire early in order to be fresh and ready for action in the morning. He briefly dismissed from his mind the fact that he had only recently committed for trial at the Crown Court an auxiliary bishop who had been charged with systematically selling off church treasures to fund his expensive inability to invest money on horses that were able to pass winning posts before many (if any) of their fellow thoroughbreds. It would be impossible that two venal clergyman would cross his path within the same month. Wouldn't it?

And anyway the hotel were at fault, not the archdeacon, and they would jolly well have to replace all his clothing and effects in the event that they were not returned to him post–haste.

So he would retire. At least, he discovered, the en suite bathroom provided sufficient facilities to enable him to do so feeling clean enough to slip under the unaccustomed duvet, without the usual security of his sensible winceyette pyjamas between himself and the sheets. It had been a battle that occupied his methodical mind for several minutes to decide whether it was better to sleep in his underwear, that he had worn all day on his journey to the Conference – or to break the habit of a lifetime and sleep unclad between the alien sheets. On balance, he decided, the latter was the more hygienic option. He listened to news on Radio 4 which he eventually was able to find on the bedside radio alarm. When the news and weather forecast concluded, he turned it off and, as was his wont, soon fell to sleep. No one would have trouble sleeping, he always maintained, if they led a blameless life. His life was beyond reproach and therefore he invariably slept soundly and usually without waking before the morning's alarm summoned him to another day of his life of industry and service. However there were occasions when he woke during the night – and this was one of them.

At two–thirty in the morning, he awoke, as he usually did if he made the mistake of consuming too much tea too late before retiring. Drowsily castigating himself for failing to remember that, half asleep, he followed the route he usually took to visit his own en–suite bathroom at home in Guildford.

Out of bed on the right hand side, two steps forward, three to the left, grope for the door handle and into the bathroom. For some reason he had never thought to question, when in the pitch black, he always shut his eyes when groping around. Maybe it was because he was protecting his eyes in the event of a protruding obstacle that might attack him at face level?

Anyway, with his eyes tight shut, as the door clicked shut behind him, he patted his hand along the wall to the left of the now closed door to find the switch that would illuminate his nocturnal relief. Unable to find the switch he opened his eyes only to discover that he was standing, stark naked, in the corridor of the hotel.

He was not a man given to any action that might be termed 'quick'. On this occasion however he turned more quickly than anyone who knew him would have thought possible and frantically tried to open the door, despite knowing, with a sickening certainty, that without that ridiculous piece of plastic that he had been given on checking in, he was not going to be able to get back into his room. He was right.

Thoughts then whirled chaotically through the rapidly clearing fog of his brain. How on earth was he to regain access to his room, without the terminal embarrassment of being seen stark naked by whichever hotel employee came to let him in?

How was he to summon assistance, anyway? He could hardly take the lift down to reception and saunter across to the desk to ask for a duplicate key. And if he knocked on another guest's door, how would they react to the sight of an unclad man with his bony hands clasped over his genitals? How would he have reacted, indeed, had the situations been reversed? There was no question of doing that; they wouldn't even wait to hear his explanation!

So – how could he get to a telephone without being seen? Before he could begin to come up with any strategy that might enable him to escape the impossible horror of his position, the sound of a clamour of excited voices approaching the junction at the top of the corridor drove him to scurry inelegantly towards a door marked "Emergency Stairs."

He made a truly bizarre sight. He was a tall man and his slenderness accentuated his height. The neat white goatee beard which he sported lent him an even more ridiculous air. He looked like nothing less than a demented great goblin from a Hans Christian Anderson story, or Don Quixote emerging from the river, as he skittered along the corridor with a jerky, stooping gait.

He had to escape before he was spotted, and wanted to protect his modesty and what remained of his dignity. He gained the sanctuary of the concrete stairwell, just in time to avoid being spotted by a five foot two Darth Vader and his girlfriend, Morgan le Fey. The incongruousness of the appearance of these two characters did not trouble their impersonators, an unemployed electrician and care assistant from Leicester. An uncharitable outsider might feel tempted to observe that the real Morgan le Fey would probably not have gained such a prodigious reputation as an irresistible enchantress had she been quite as massive as her 21st Century impersonator and furthermore would probably have been less inclined to allow cleavage to dominate all her other undoubted qualities quite so comprehensively.

These uncharitable thoughts did not however occupy Leslie. He had more important things to think about. He had to find a telephone. He descended to the next floor and cautiously opened the door into an identical corridor to that on the seventh floor he had just left. It would be pointless to emerge from his temporary safe refuge in the stairwell unless there were something visible in the corridor that might offer him a solution to his hideous problem. And the only solution he could come up with – was a telephone!

Similarly, the sixth and fifth floors offered no solace as a rising panic began to make his heart hammer uncomfortably in his throat and he felt the sweat of terror stinging in his eyes. He was getting further and further away from his room, the room that he was now beginning to see as the only point of safety in a frightening and dangerous world.

He then reasoned that the likeliest spot to find a telephone, without the risk of being seen before he could summon assistance, was in the basement. In the basement, the kitchen and maintenance staff were bound to need to be able to contact the switchboard for any number of reasons. And that would be mainly, of course, during the day. Maybe if he were able to get down there now, when no one was likely to be working there, he could access such a phone. A glimmer of hope drove him on and further down the staircase. As he passed the exit door to each floor on the way down, he was constantly made aware that there were many infuriating, merry-making residents still roaming the corridors. Distant laughter and bursts of artificial laser fire, mingled with electronically distorted voices, served to remind Leslie that he was still in imminent danger of the most unwelcome experience of what he, at least, regarded as his hitherto entirely blameless life.

After several heart-stoppingly close calls, he reached the deserted hinterland of the service areas of the basement and saw a sight that in his predicament was comparable to an oasis to a parched traveller in the wastes of the Sahara at midday, a glorious Bakelite telephone attached to the wall beside a row of aluminium trolleys, bearing stacks of clean crockery.

As he grasped the handset with relief, and his hand was poised to dial 100, a pair of doors crashed open and two alien monsters came through, firing burst of staccato electronic 'fire' back into the room they had left, to the accompaniment of cheers of encouragement from those within. Before the revellers could turn and behold the unlikely sight of the crouching, naked and horrified Justice of the Peace, church warden and founder member of the Guildford Guardians of Decency, Leslie had ducked into an open doorway. He found himself in a store room which was the temporary repository of assorted artefacts, weapons and other items belonging to the convention organisers, including a Cyberman costume and a Dalek. It was being used, with the agreement of the hotel, as a safe storage for items which might tempt the less scrupulous fan to purloin them; items that were highly desirable collectors' pieces.

Under normal circumstances, Leslie would rather have died than assume any of these disguises; but at this moment, the role of a Cyberman seemed a very attractive alternative to his present vulnerable situation. All he had to do was clamber into the costume, then walk openly, without exciting any comment, to the front desk, explain the situation and have the porter re-admit him to his room.

He lifted the silver painted wellington boots off the rubberised, tube encrusted boiler suit but, before he could pick the suit itself up, he heard one of the two gun-toting aliens approaching the entrance to his sanctuary say

"C'mon Brian, let's get the stuff up to the main room. Andrew'll do a queenie strop if it's not all set up for the opening ceremonies in the morning, and, I don't know about you, but I don't fancy doing it all at the crack of dawn!"

Leslie's instinct for shame avoidance drove him to make his next big mistake. Still clutching the silver gumboots, he climbed inside the Dalek and pulled the hinged domed lid down over his head.

Later, when going over the sequence of events that had occurred that fateful night, he realised that if anyone might just have been likely to accept his story and sympathise with his plight, it could well have been these two young men, who evidently inhabited a world in which nude men skulking furtively in basements would not perhaps excite the same reaction as they undoubtedly would in the less imaginative and liberal world that Leslie inhabited.

However, all these thoughts came later. Much later.

Leslie was now sitting naked inside a Dalek, clutching a pair of rubber boots. He was being wheeled through the still busy foyer of an hotel in the small hours of the morning by two young men dressed as alien monsters. As he passed out of the reception area, he thought of shouting out for assistance, but could not help but imagine the likely reaction of the young girl behind the counter and the dozen or so people he could see through the grill on the front of the Dalek, who sprawled chatting in groups around the low tables, that were littered with the debris of a night's carousing. The Dalek was pushed by the young men across the car park and through the formal garden in front of the hotel into the Conference centre some hundred or so yards from the main hotel.

A half an hour later, he was alone in the main hall, inside a Dalek and heard the night porter incongruously assuring the two alien monsters that the room would be securely locked until they came to him and requested it to be opened in the morning. (Yes, he would still be on duty – he was always on duty. He was shamefully overworked. The hotel industry gave no protection for its workers!)

He was alone. Leslie climbed out of the Dalek and frantically searched the hall for anything with which he might cover himself with any measure of dignity before attempting once again to summon assistance.

There was nothing. Absolutely nothing.

In desperation, he put on the silvered rubber wellington boots, and removed from a table on the stage an alien mask which, although he neither knew nor indeed would he have cared, had been used in 'Star Trek – The Next Generation'. Holding it strategically in front of him with one hand, and a broken chair back behind him with the other, he explored the room in the dim emergency lighting and found a pair of fire doors with push bars on the wall opposite the entrance. He contemplated his options and found that at this point there were none, other than what he was about to do. So he pushed slowly on the horizontal bars and the doors crashed open.

He emerged from the warmth of the hotel into the darkness of a narrow paved walkway, surrounded with gravel that ran along the back of the hotel.

Events seemed now to take place without any further input from the exhausted and sorry spectacle that Leslie had now become. As if in a trance, he arrived at the rear corner of the building to peer round before embarking into another unknown realm. With a sudden surge of hope, he saw that there was a public telephone kiosk on the pavement at the side of the road that ran up the western perimeter of the hotel. All he had to do was climb the grassy bank and make his way through a clump of low bushes. He would even be able to reach the telephone from the security of those very bushes without exposing himself to the gaze of any passing motorist. Clutching the mask before him and abandoning the chair back in order to use his hand to scrabble up the slope, he climbed awkwardly up the bank. As he gingerly negotiated his painful path through the evergreen and holly bushes that separated him from his lifeline to a world of normalcy and safety, the world erupted into madness.

Simultaneously quartz halogen spotlights sprang on all around the hotel, a young courting couple in considerable disarray sprang to their feet from the bushes only feet away from him and a police car screeched to a standstill beside the very telephone kiosk towards which he had been making his painful way.

The police had been summoned by the triggering of the security alarm when he had opened the crash doors in the main exhibition hall.

Dazzled by the lights coming at him from all directions, Leslie understandably, but ill–advisedly in the circumstances, lifted the mask to his face to shield his eyes from the glare.

"Now listen, this isn't what it seems, officer."

"Isn't it sir? Well, then there's a novelty!" replied one of the policeman as his colleague returned to their squad car to get a blanket to wrap around Leslie.

His concern, it must be understood was not for Leslie's comfort, but for the sensibilities of himself and his colleague and anyone else who might have to gaze upon the capering pervert that was protesting to his fellow officer "There is a perfectly logical explanation for all this, officer. There is no need for you to trouble yourselves unduly. Just escort me back to the hotel would you – and we can sort all this out."

"We will certainly be escorting you sir, but to a nice warm cell in the police station. Here, wrap this around yourself, please – and give me that – er – head thing – whatever it is."

"What? Don't be ridiculous, officer. You don't understand. Look, I'm a magistrate, for heaven's sake!"

"Were you sir?" came the chilling reply.

The following day Leslie appeared in the local magistrates' court and at the end of the proceedings, as if through a fog and a very long way off, he heard the doughty and implacable lady magistrate begin:

"I never cease to be amazed at the brazen effrontery…"

Carter's First Case

Carter Battersby was perplexed.

Three short weeks earlier, he had been sent for an interview by the Job Centre. At his first visit, when he filled in the forms about his employment preferences, he had specified "Private Investigator, Detection and Undercover Work" as absolutely the only job that he was prepared to accept. As a result of this clever ruse, he had expected to have several trouble free months, if not years, living off income support and as many other state benefits as he could garner before being forced to accept the inconvenience of proper employment once again. The world of employment had thus far not appealed to him overmuch. He had not enjoyed working in the men's outfitters in the department store in the high street. His co–workers were a mean spirited bunch, whose sole delight seemed to be in setting him up for ever more complicated embarrassments and humiliations in front of employer and customers alike. Their amusement at their prey's discomfiture led them to persuade friends to come in and accuse him of taking their measurements down incorrectly at a previous visit when another friend had come in to be measured. When he discovered what they had done he had lost his rag and unfortunately the cup of coffee he threw at his main tormentor had damaged a cashmere coat awaiting collection by a valued customer. He had not enjoyed working for the Refuse Disposal Department's Transport Office either, and the feeling was definitely mutual. He and his immediate superior were, it cannot be denied, congenitally programmed to be incompatible. Samuel Butterworth was a man who liked a well–filled in form, an empty in–tray and compliance with procedural niceties much more than he liked anything else that he could think of, as his family would readily attest, as well as those who worked in his department. Carter Battersby viewed forms, in–trays and procedural niceties in much the same way as a goat views the barbed wire that separates him from those lovely flower beds on the other side – as a considerable inconvenience to be circumvented by any means possible.

Carter was affable, fond of his fellow man, provided they didn't take the mick or interfere with his tendency to 'chillax' whenever possible, and he certainly knew how to enjoy his leisure. These characteristics are not entirely welcome in any workplace. But a Refuse Disposal Department's Transport Office under the eagle eye of Samuel Butterworth was certainly not a naturally ideal environment for one of Carter's disposition. The collection days scheduled for three dustcarts and their teams did not match the new information sent to the householders on those rounds. The result was that those dustcarts returned early and empty on successive days, bearing their contented 'jobsworth' drivers and loaders – who, having been repeatedly instructed not to go in search of bins that were not placed outside their properties at the appointed collection time, were only too delighted to oblige. Only those householders who had failed to collect their bins the previous week received the benefit of the dustmen's attentions – and most of those were empty anyway. Nothing, it seems, infuriates a householder more than having their rubbish ignored and left to fester and accumulate insolently outside their homes, prey to the depredations of foxes and small boys of a mischievous disposition. Mr. Butterworth needed only a short investigation to discover the sole and seemingly unrepentant cause of all his infuriating ear–bashing from a horde of Council Tax payers of variable politeness was Carter the careless. Carter the feckless. Carter the instantly jobless.

Carter himself had discovered as a result of this process that he was not, as he explained to his friends in the pub later, a 'corporate person'.

"I'm not like you nine to fivers. I mean I wish I was, in a way. It would make life easier, I suppose. But because I'm not, I don't want to be. I want to break free, as some great poet once said."

"You mean 'as Freddie Mercury once sang', don't you?" asked his friend, George who worked in a music shop and loved his job and whilst he knew how lucky he was to get the job of his dreams, he was not inclined to feel any sympathy for his friend at that moment, seeing him as at best a lazy blighter and at worst a sponger on society.

"Well yeah, alright.... Queen may have quoted it. They were always doing that. But a poet wrote it... must have done – 'cause it sums up the human condition, doesn't it? You can be a poet without writing Gray's thingy in a country whatsit, can't you?" he added emphatically, without any awareness of the inherent limpness of his retort.

George stared at him for a moment and decided not to pursue that particular strand of conversation.

"Well, I don't know about you, but my human condition is in need of another drink and it's your round Carter, so you can use your Income Support money to get them in!"

It was to Carter's great irritation then, that a few days later, he was asked to attend an interview for a job with "Percy Tucker (Investigations) – Confidentiality Guaranteed." His irritation, (not to mention surprise) after casually giving a deliberately fairly lack–lustre performance at his interview, (although it was debatable whether he could have done any better, had he actually been trying to get the job) was magnified when he was offered the job. The sole proprietor of the business, the ailing Percy, was desperate and had not warmed to the only other applicant for the post, a police officer with the eyes of dead carp and the body odour to match, who had taken early retirement after too many confessions had been found to emanate from bruised prisoners with a hunted look. Percy knew that to allow this candidate anywhere near his agency would have resulted in mayhem and Percy was in no fit state to deal with mayhem at that particular time in his life.

So Carter was employed as a private investigator's assistant and simple curiosity had led him to turn up on time and see what happened. After all you never knew, it might be a good laugh and Percy seemed a harmless and amiable enough old chap.

The last three weeks since he had started working for Percy, had been eventful and, to Carter's surprise, quite interesting. His first assignment had been remarkably simple and, more importantly in Percy's eyes, successful. He had followed an erring husband for ten days and obtained photographic evidence of his alfresco activities with a strapping fitness instructor of uncertain gender. The wronged spouse, on confirming her worst suspicions, had been more than generous in the light of her sudden access to sole occupancy of the house she loved combined with the wherewithal to maintain it in the manner she liked, without having to tolerate any more of her soon to be ex–husband's parsimony and 'appetites'. The delighted Percy had passed on a part of the unexpected bonus to Carter, who at that moment started to believe that this might indeed be a job that was suited to the talents he was suddenly believing he might actually possess.

His current task was staking out an allotment in order to trap a nocturnal dahlia nobbler in the weeks leading up to an annual village show, where rivalries over the flower and vegetable section had forced the organisers to ship in judges from another county in order to protect them from reprisals from the outraged nurturer of the second best tomato or chrysanthemum. Carter had been surprised to learn quite how passionate the gentle art of horticulture could become when it was not just the fingers that were green, but the owners of those fingers when confronted with a superior pelargonium or straighter asparagus spear.

It had all therefore been quite painless and even enjoyable until poor old Percy succumbed to his third heart–attack while sitting in front of the television watching 'Road Wars' one night. His last words apparently were "Probation? Probation!!!? Six cars totalled, a police car in a ditch, no licence or insurance and the little toe–rag gets probation. I know what I'd do! I'd...." Alas, even though his wife Dorothy knew pretty much what Percy had in mind for the serial offending and unrepentant hoodie, she was never to hear the detail of this particular planned retribution.

At the wake after the funeral, Carter was surprised when she implored him to carry on the business. He had thought that his thitherto firmly held desire for continuous state support was going to be granted, which would have been an ironic twist given the fact that for the first time in his life he was actually beginning to feel useful and fulfilled. The grieving Dorothy, it transpired, had no other means of financial support. Percy had had many qualities; he had been a dutiful and caring husband and, whilst not in the forefront of his industry, had managed over the years to provide for his wife and himself adequately if not spectacularly. However, he had never been that savvy financially and whenever he saw the word 'pension', his first thoughts were of their occasional forays to France to get cheap fags and booze, which they both turned into a short holiday where they stayed in the ubiquitous boarding houses of that name. The other kind, where you saved up for an uncertain old age never really seemed to him that good an idea. And in the event, of course, from his own, albeit selfish, point of view he was in inarguably correct. It hadn't worked out quite as well (financially anyway) for Dorothy, however. She had helped her husband out with the paperwork and admin tasks that beset all small businesses but she had neither the personality nor the experience to carry on the business alone. Nor was she likely to find another job that might enable her to keep up even her modest lifestyle.

She was nonetheless of a more practical disposition than her late husband, so she made Carter an offer that she desperately hoped he would find impossible to resist. Being a long term member of the local amateur theatrical society, she knew how to work a sympathetic audience. She was undoubtedly genuinely bereaved and had loved old Percy to bits, but she was also a practical woman and knew that the task of securing her future now lay firmly and exclusively in her own hands. She gave her performance of a lifetime. She poured him another glass of beer and as she pressed it into his hand, she allowed one tear to roll down her cheek. Just one, no more. She had a fine sense of well–judged understatement; a characteristic that was a significant rarity in the amateur drama circles in which she moved. She put on her brave face and told him that the bread and butter work was regular and undeniably sufficient to support them both and that she was prepared to give him sixty percent of both the profits and the capital value of the premises and goodwill. A lesser woman would have kept the lion's share of the business for herself, but Dorothy was a shrewd judge of both character and the way things were. She had seen a glimmer of something in Carter that others had missed. She saw a quality that she would have liked to have seen in any son she might have had herself. She and Percy had been childless. They had not intended not to have children nor had they set out to have them. They had tacitly left it to nature and nature had simply not obliged.

One of Dorothy's qualities was one that she probably didn't even realise she had. She had an instinctive need and desire to please other people and so, throughout her life, had been unfailingly able to see the other person's point of view. She therefore was ideally placed to correctly judge both Carter and the needs of their respective current situations.

He was unable to resist both the very generous terms of her offer and the romantic vision of himself as the twenty-three year old sleuth, protector of widows and prowling denizen of the twilight world of crime, the darkest corners of which he would illuminate with his flaming sword of righteous truth. Or words to that flaming effect. As a regular player of computer games where heroes are given mighty tasks and achieve them by pitting their wits and muscles against the most terrifying adversaries, he relished the opportunity to live out those fantasies in the real and less scary world that he inhabited, where the wit and muscle quotient, he anticipated, would be exponentially lower.

But now that the dust had settled and, after many uncomfortable nights crouched behind the compost heaps with only his newly acquired Nintendo DS as company, he had identified and exposed the dastardly dahlia nobbler. The nocturnal miscreant was in fact a retired solicitor, no less, who had been, as a result, ceremoniously blacklisted by the local horticultural society and unceremoniously shunned by the rest of the local population before eventually moving to the outskirts of Birmingham where no one knew of his misdeeds. So Carter suddenly found himself confronted with a proper case and didn't know where to begin. The widow, Dorothy, had phoned to ask him to go post–haste to the home of a friend, who was prepared to pay most handsomely for a very swift resolution to a highly confidential and awkward domestic problem.

"The Ponderosa", the home of the aforesaid friend, was a spectacular example of the pseudo–hacienda style of architecture favoured by those blessed with a great deal more money than taste. The profusion of marble, gilt and garish art would have even have looked grotesque in those parts of the world whose architectural styles the unfortunate architect was trying to emulate at the misguided behest of his clients. Here in the leafy suburbs, its hideousness was magnified to such a point that any reaction to its sheer awfulness was frankly pointless. Carter, of course, having little taste, was quite impressed. He didn't know much about art but he had a good idea what ownership of great big gold framed pictures, combined with marble and more gold things, probably meant. If that's what people who had shed loads of dosh thought was the bee's knees, then it was okay by him. Bring it on.

"You're a bit young aren't you love?" said Trish Potter, surveying the skinny frame that Carter inhabited and his unruly mop of reddish hair. Trish Potter looked as if she had just stepped out of a film into the real world. Not the kind of film however that might spring to everyone's mind when they were searching for an example of glamour or sophistication. Trish, bless her, was more reminiscent of those ladies that an amorous window cleaner might have very good reason for thinking was likely to deflect him away from his chamois leather and bucket for a while, if he wasn't (or was?) careful. However, because he was indeed 'a bit young', and more innocent than he might like to think of himself during his daydreams about the adventures of a private eye, these thoughts did not cross Carter's mind in any helpful way. He had never had to deal with anyone like Trish before and wasn't quite sure how to start now.

"Well, I..." he began.

"Never mind, dear" she interrupted benignly, "Dotty says you know what you're on about, and old Percy – God rest his soul, what a lovely feller he was – wouldn't have taken you on if you didn't, would he, eh?"

Trish Potter hitched the pink housecoat together over her ample, brown, freckled bosom and continued in a conspiratorial tone leaning towards him so that he could smell her breath that smelt of lipstick and gin, "It's a matter of life and death, Carter. You don't mind if I call you 'Carter', do you?"

"No, that's fine, I...."

"Only I'd feel funny calling a young chap like you 'Mr Battersby.' Anyway, you see, Carter, – it's a very delicate matter and I need your absolute discretion. You know what I mean? Hmmm? Discretion with a capital D, dear. My Bernard would do his nut if he found out, and I daren't call the police because I don't know whether it's... well, you know, on the level with the tax and the VAT and all that , if you see what I mean, and my Bernard wouldn't like to give that lot an excuse to go prowling around his affairs, know what I mean?" she repeated.

She paused expectantly, looking at him for some confirmation of his familiarity with the delicate niceties of the black economy. She didn't receive it.

"Er, no, I'm afraid I don't. Sorry Mrs. Potter, but... er, what is it you daren't call the police about, exactly? You haven't told me what it is that you want me to do."

"It's my coat, love – my lovely Russian Sable – didn't Dotty tell you? Oh she probably thought it was better coming from me. Anyway, it's gone. I was only out for half an hour. He'll go ape–whatsit if he finds out. I left the bedroom window open. It was stupid of me I know. I noticed when I came back up the drive; I ran upstairs to check and it was gone. He's always goin' on and on like a bleedin' record about security and alarms – but I was only going down to the main road to the chemist for my repeat prescription of tranquillisers. You can help me can't you?"

Her fingers dug so hard into his upper arms that he yelped with pain and surprise.

"Yes, of course, Mrs. Potter. Well, I'll do my best of course..."

Spotting her look of frenzied anxiety, he changed tack swiftly. Carter lacked many social skills and high on the list of his inadequacies in that area was the ability to deal with

hysterical women. He wanted to avoid that at all costs, even if in the event he was merely generating an even worse reaction that would surface (even less manageably) later.
He adopted a tone of assured confidence that surprised him as much as her with its even, confident tone.

"I'll do more than that: I'll get it back for you. Don't worry, Mrs. Potter. You just leave everything to me. It's my job and your satisfaction is my ultimate objective!"

"I'll do anything to get that coat back before tonight, Carter, absolutely anything! I told dear Dotty, you can name your price!"

"Well I charge out of pocket expenses, obviously, plus an hourly rate of..."

She wasn't interested in the fine detail. She wanted action and, in her experience, action was always forthcoming when large wads of readies were thrown at whatever might be perceived to be a problem.

"I'll give you a grand, in cash, Carter, if that coat is back in my closet before my Bernard comes home tonight! There's a photo of me wearing it at the premiere of the latest Bond film on the white baby grand over there, so you know what it looks like. Take the picture if you have to, but put it back after or my Bernard'll notice. He don't miss nothing. Mind you, I shouldn't think there are too many top grade Russian sables lying around unclaimed or being offered for readies in the local pubs, so you won't be 'avin' the problem of deciding which of several Russian sables it is. I'm not interested in getting anyone in trouble with the Old Bill and if you have to buy the ruddy thing back, fair enough – put it on expenses. Whatever you have to do, Carter – do it. Look I've got my personal trainer waiting for me in the pool complex..." (she used those words in the same way as he would have said 'in the kitchen', he noticed in a kind of mute awe) "... and I'd better carry on as if everything's alright. No point in getting' anyone chattin' or gossipin' is there? So I'll just leave it all to you. Have a good look round. I'll be in all day. Let me know as soon as you have any news, won't you Carter? And give me a shout if you need any more information, won't you? And above all – discretion, Carter, discretion! I am relying on you, mind! And I'll be very, very grateful... I really will...."

She then clattered up the stairs with him to show him the scene of the crime in the dressing room, adjacent to their heavily mirrored and very fluffy bedroom before disappearing for her appointment with physical exhaustion.

Carter started by going over to the open window and examining it carefully. Having examined it for a good ten minutes, from inside and out and every angle, he felt that nothing more was to be gained by staring blankly at a very ordinary window which bore no tell–tale shreds of clothing or bloodstains or indeed of anything much, other than high gloss paint and, of course, glass. Even the glass was clean and devoid of any smear or smudges, let alone fingerprints. He then gave the same degree of attention to the clothes cupboard and the polished floor in between it and the aforesaid window. He looked under the bed, more in hope than expectation. He came back downstairs and went right round the outside of the house until he found himself under the open window that had led to the loss of the sable. No train ticket, monogrammed cap or wallet lodged in the bushes below. No footprint in the soft earth that might send him looking for a one legged man or a felonious cricketer. No marks of a ladder. It seemed to Carter's (admittedly very inexpert) eye that no–one had recently entered through that window. Yet, the coat was certainly not in the cupboard, as the very empty silk padded hanger had borne eloquent testimony.

What on earth now? Ask the neighbours? You never know, he thought, suppressing the leaden certainty that he did, in fact, know very well indeed.

"Can you tell Mrs. Potter that I'm just going to have a word with some of her neighbours and ask them if they saw anyone suspicious hanging around this morning and – er – we'll take it from there," he explained in an attempt to convey information via the impassive cleaner, who probably hadn't understand a single word he had said, as was evidenced by the fact that she said "Sank you please yes?" as he headed out of the iron studded, oak–effect front door.

Quite what he could do if the neighbours had by chance noticed something, he didn't know.

Eight suspicious neighbours later, Carter was no closer to anything resembling a lead. Trying to elicit information from third parties about something that he knew needed to be kept as confidential as possible was no easy task. Naturally many of the neighbours in their more traditional homes in this leafy suburb were not particularly well disposed to their garish, noisy neighbours and were anxious to find out why this strange young man was asking them if they had noticed anything strange going on.

Walking away from the last of the houses under the eagle eye of the retired army officer who lived there, Carter considered his plight.

"What would Peter Wimsey do now? Or Sam Spade?" he mused gloomily, as he got into his car and sat in despair. At that moment he saw a gleaming black limousine glide up to the gates that opened onto the The Ponderosa's long white gravelled drive. The only occupant, a uniformed chauffeur, glanced up and down the road somewhat furtively, thought Carter as he sat unnoticed in the shadow cast by the elm trees that lined the road. The chauffeur then sidled into the bushes and undergrowth on the right hand side of the drive and emerged seconds later carrying a black plastic bin bag, which he placed carefully on the front seat of the car before speeding smoothly off.

"Oh, yes! Here we go my little beauty..." thought Carter, thanking whoever was the patron saint of inexperienced investigators as he fired up the engine of the firm's Fiat Uno. "It must be. I can see it all – a gentleman cracksman, dressed from head to foot in black, must have slipped in and out of The Ponderosa, swinging in through the window on nylon wire, leaving no trace as he half inched the fur coat and then stashed the loot for his accomplice – who had served as his batman in the army – to collect at leisure when the heat was off. Yes! My son! Yes!"

Carter had never tailed anyone before. For the first time since he had inherited the Uno along with the business, he was grateful that his vehicle was quite so non–descript. Until now he would have preferred something along the lines of a BMW or better still one of those American cars that bounced so wonderfully across the junctions in those American car chase films. But for this particular 'operation' he was grateful not to be an exciting sight in the rear view mirror of the Bentley that sped along in front of him.

It was, in fact, surprisingly easy, despite the odd worrying moment when vehicles slipped in between them at roundabouts and intersections.

If Carter had been a little more experienced in his new profession, it is probable that he would not have followed the limo right into the car park at the back of the hangar-like building at the far end of the trading estate. But, if the chauffeur had at any point registered his presence behind him, he gave no indication of it.

Carter put on his sunglasses ('shades, natch!') and watched from his car, as a thickset grey haired man in a shiny suit bustled down a fire–escape at the back of the building and was handed the plastic sack. He opened it and immediately hurled it on the ground in rage. The bag burst open, spilling its messy contents over the asphalt. Clearly teabags, Crunchy Nut Cornflakes packets and potato peelings were not what he was expecting to find. Nor were they what Carter was hoping to see. Shiny–suit, by now somewhat redder in the face, then vigorously berated clearly crestfallen chauffeur uniform, whose body language gave every indication of the aggrieved innocence of a minion doing his best in difficult circumstances. They then both got back into the limo, which swung out of the car park, in the direction, Carter suspected, of The Ponderosa, yet again.

Carter's first piece of real detection was a mixture of intuition and pure unadulterated, copper bottomed luck. Instead of doing what might have seemed obvious and sticking close to his only lead - the departing Bentley and its occupants - he gambled on a hunch and headed for the waste disposal site at Barley Hill. Such hunches are what separate the true sleuth from the mundane. Serendipity had thrust the hunch in Carter's direction and he knew a sable coloured road when he saw it.

Twenty minutes later he was standing, as his mother would say "like Piffy on a monument", on top of a mountain of black plastic bags. His former career with the Refusal Disposal Department, albeit brief, had left him with some friendly contacts at Barley Hill. Whilst those in the admin office (which was, of course, as far away from the inconvenient aromas of the fruit of their official labours as possible) had little or no time for their erstwhile clerk, at the sharp end of the operation there were quite a few who were disposed to view favourably anyone who gave any kind of grief to the pen pushers and paper clip wielders who dossed their lives away in the comfort of the heated and carpeted offices of the Town Hall. So when Carter had turned up, whipped his shades off and produced his Private Eye I.D., instead of telling him to do something inelegant with them, they gave him a slap on the back and cordially invited him to make free with the multiple manifestations of their malodorous product. They indicated to him on the wall–chart in the hut that served as an office where the day's discharge point had been and supplied him with the regulation hard hat, as required by the great God 'Helfensayfty'. They then left him to his own devices as they disappeared into their portakabin for the umpteenth cuppa of the day. He drove down the track made by the tractors across the across the uneven terrain site to the eastern edge of the land fill site and, fortified by a promise of no further waste tipping in that area that afternoon, began his messy and frankly daunting search. Forty–five increasingly dispiriting and frustrating minutes after that, he stood up triumphantly holding in his arms a coat that would have reduced anti–fur lobbyists to an apoplexy of righteous indignation. As the grin of success against the odds spread across his refuse spattered face, he heard a voice bellowing behind him. A voice that he instinctively recognised as belonging to someone who was not in the habit of being ignored

"Before you get any big ideas son, – that's my property you've got there – go and get it Harry." It was the man he had seen doing the tarantella on the bag of rubbish on the trading estate and Harry was the chauffeur who had provoked his merry dance by delivering the bag. As Harry advanced towards him purposefully but carefully across the mound of opened black plastic bags that attested to the frenzy of Carter's long search, the young detective decided to play the only card he had.

He took a deep breath.

"I'm afraid, you're mistaken, gentlemen. First of all under the byelaws of this borough, any item found on this tip is the property of the council, until any other claimant's lawful right of title is established through the appropriate channels. I am a Private Investigator, who has been charged with the burden of locating this item and this coat is the property of my instructing client. I must ask you to let me pass or I shall be obliged to take the matter further," he finished, feeling rather proud of himself, both for his detailed grasp of the legal niceties and for what he saw as the firm and authoritative, no nonsense manner of his delivery of that information.

"I don't care if you're Sherlock bloody Holmes, lad. That coat is mine, whatever your 'client' says." He spoke the word as if it meant something even less appetising than what you might find on the bottom of your shoe. "And," he continued imperturbably, "you'll get a sound smackin', son, if you don't hand it over to Harry, pronto!"

"Better do what Mr. Potter says, son" offered Harry helpfully, "He doesn't make idle threats."

"Mr Potter! Oh! No..." started Carter before he was cut off by the former's bellowed response.

"Shut your stupid mouth, Harry, no names no pack drill, eh!" shouted the now firmly identified and hacked–off Bernard Potter.

"Is Trish Potter your wife?" blurted Carter.

"Eh? What d'you mean? What's that got to do with you? What's goin' on 'ere you little toe–rag? Just what the 'ell are you doin' with that coat – and how did you know it belonged to my wife?"

In the face of two rather formidable looking men, who could quite easily have used him as a practice trampoline had the whim taken them, Carter had no option but to do the one thing that he had been asked not to do and explain to Bernard, the husband of his worried and fearful client, the details of his mission. Obviously, he surmised, Bernard Potter knew of the coat's absence from its proper place on the padded rail in the fluffy bedroom of many mirrors at The Ponderosa, so there was no logical way in which he could be expected to protect his client any more. He decided to come clean and at least hope to avoid the worst manifestations of the promised 'smacking' which, looking at the two stony faced men facing him, he had no reason to believe would be other than comprehensive and efficient. They listened carefully to his story.

When Carter finished and opened his arms out in a gesture of surrender, in the hope of placating the two men, there was a long pause before Bernard Potter pursed his lips thoughtfully and gave a low whistle.

"Right, son. I see. Thank you for being honest with me. That puts a different complexion on things, as it happens. Fear not. All will be well if you do exactly what I say. What I want you to do is this..."

A little while later, Carter was sitting in the biggest sitting room he had ever seen, with a cup of tea and a bourbon biscuit in front of him, explaining to his anxious client that he had found a couple of very strong leads indeed and was confident that he could recover the coat within three days at the most. He was unable to give her any more information at the moment, as he had to protect his sources in both the criminal world and – "Er, 'other' places," he added mysteriously, in the fond hope that she might think he was able to tap into the security services at will. Trish was not interested in the minutiae of his investigation. Results were the only thing that concerned her and she had been offered a temporary respite, it seemed.

"Well, son, as it turns out," replied Trish, now dressed in a peach coloured trouser suit with embroidered panda motifs, "that may be just hunky dory. Bernard's just phoned. He's away on business 'til the weekend. Just as long as it's back before then... I'll be so grateful, dear Carter! Keep me posted, dear? Oh, and I'll have the picture back if you don't need it any more. Just stick it on the baby grand before you go. 'Scuse me Carter if I rush off, won't you – as Bernard's away for a couple of days I'm off out with the girls tonight for a bit of a bop. Bernard don't like dancin', so I'm taking the opportunity. Do you salsa, Carter?"

He shook his head warily.

"You should. It's great exercise and a young chap like you should get those muscles toned up. You're not a bad lookin' lad you know. The girls down the Salsa club'd go mad for you. Carter....." she threw over her shoulder as she shimmied off to go and prepare for the night of freedom from the domineering and presumably salsa avoiding Bernard.

It seemed that Bernard Potter had cash flow problems. He needed forty thousand pounds in cash urgently and the coat could raise it painlessly and swiftly with the promise of similarly swift and painless redemption, if the deal that he had been carefully nurturing for some time went through satisfactorily, a few days later.

He had stashed the coat in a bin bag by the gate for his chauffeur, Harry to collect. However the refuse collection had been made a day early, because of the impending Bank Holiday at the weekend and Harry had picked up the bag of fresh rubbish taken out later by the cleaner.

Carter's brief sojourn with the waste disposal department had not only provided him with the knowledge of that early bank holiday collection, but had led him to the right tip at the right place, ahead of Bernard Potter and, even more importantly for all concerned, before the precious coat had been buried under tons of waste.

Bernard handed the coat over to Carter three days later and, having done extremely well on his unspecified (and probably best forgotten) deal pressed £500 into his hand with a conspiratorial wink. "Mum's the word, son. I know a smart young lad like you understands how these things work – and you've met Trish, so you know that I like to keep her happy! And you never know, I might be able to put some work your way in the future, if you show me how discreet you can be? Eh? Know what I mean son?"

The grateful Trish, who brushed aside Carter's modest mutterings about "routine procedures" and "all in a day's work", gave him the promised £1,000 fee, plus a bonus of £100 for expenses – which he gratefully accepted after muttering diffidently about £5.00 for petrol being more than enough. She told him that she would call her friend Dorothy and tell just what a little treasure she had taken on and that her business would be more than safe in Carter's capable hands. And if he ever wanted to meet some of her nice young friends down the dance club for a spot of salsa, she'd send her Bernard's chauffeur over to pick him up.

"Just give me a call, Carter dear. I know you'd have fun!"

"Well," thought Carter, as he adopted a nonchalant pose in front of the office mirror that evening, "at least it will keep me going until that mysterious leggy blonde with the black veil staggers in and faints in my arms. He threw his hat at the hook on the wall and for the first time ever it landed perfectly and hung there as if to salute the new detective on the block. And sadly there was no one there to see it – and he knew it would never happen again. He was right about that at least.

A Matter of Form

"Pop down to the Law Stationers and pick up a hundred Oral Agreement Forms, would you Martin? Put them on our account."

It was Martin Slocombe's first day as an articled clerk.

Martin's father had given him every opportunity to choose a sensible career and had listened attentively as Martin expressed an interest in working in what he described as "the media". In particular, he explained, he saw himself as a copywriter for a high powered advertising agency churning out pithy one–liners, or as a television presenter, reading an autocue and interviewing pop stars on Saturday morning television. He knew that if he just had the right opportunities, he could thrive in that field of work.

Having nodded understandingly and appearing to give due consideration to each utterance while Martin outlined his ambitious but vague plans, his father paused only briefly before informing him that he had, at great cost to himself of time and energy, called in a favour and arranged articles for him at his Company's Solicitors' office. If he wished to continue living under the same roof and have his poor mother continue to cook, wash and clean for him, he might very well consider a career with better prospects than the airy fairy world he had just described, and for which Martin was demonstrably totally unsuitable. Martin had no real chance to register more than a half–hearted protest. His father had always had the ability to quell any hint of rebellion, or indeed discussion, with a single look. Martin decided to give the law a go and rapidly shifted his erstwhile fantasy future into another mode – that of the campaigning lawyer. Like the hero of his childhood, the indomitable 'Just William', he would "right wrongs". For some obscure reason, he considered that this was the ambition of all members of the legal profession. The rest of us live in the real world and realise, of course, that the principal objective of the legal profession is to manipulate and manoeuvre the intricacies and contradictions of the law to the advantage of their clients, in return for shovels full of coin of the realm. There are of course exceptions to this rule as, indeed, there are accountants who spend their spare time being "stand-up comedians" and doing hilarious routines on the alternative comedy circuit and politicians who answer every question fully and in great detail on every occasion.

Martin had been given the guided tour of the office. He had been introduced to all the partners and the other articled clerks. He had been taken into the room occupied by their secretaries who looked at him carefully to see what sort he was likely to be. Was he the confident cocky type who patronised them and tried to get the prettier and younger ones to go and have a drink with them after work? Or was he one of the wet behind the ears ones who didn't have a clue about life, the law or women. It didn't take the secretaries long to place Martin firmly in the latter category. The senior partner, to whom he had been attached, had then sent him for a briefing by the office manager, Sam Coppock, the man who really ran the office and to whom the partners all deferred in the tricky business of seeing that a building staffed by some forty people ran smoothly and effectively. After a run-down of basic office procedures, Martin had been given his first task as a fledgling would–be solicitor: to go and fetch a hundred oral agreement forms from the Law Stationers.

Menial though the errand might be, he was determined to make a swift impression by demonstrating his speed, willingness and efficiency. He was down the stairs and into the street, repeating the instruction to himself – "…a hundred oral agreement forms from the Law Stationers, a hundred oral agreement forms from…" He stopped –

a sudden realisation struck him. He raised eyes his to heaven and groaned, before turning round and slowly re–tracing his steps.

"You must think me an awful twerp, Mr. Coppock!"

"Must I, Martin? Don't I have any choice in the matter? Oh well, if you so wish, I shall endeavour to regard you in the way you describe. Perhaps you could help me arrive at this low opinion of you by suggesting some reason for your 'awful twerp–dom'?"

Martin stared blankly back at him. "Er, I'm sorry, I don't quite... Oh right, yes... I see!" He gave a short laugh.

"Well, you just asked me to go to the Law Stationers and collect a hundred Oral Agreement forms!" said Martin, shaking his head in disbelief at his own stupidity.

"Ye–es?" replied Sam Coppock, expectantly. Perhaps, just perhaps, this one might be showing promising signs of intelligence, unlike the majority of his predecessors. Maybe it wouldn't take six months to house train this one.

"Well I was so keen to get on with the job, that I was half way down the street practically before it dawned on me." he paused, smacked his forehead and gave an exaggerated laugh at his own stupidity. "How can I possibly get a hundred Oral Agreement Forms from the Law Stationers, when I haven't got the faintest clue where the 'Law Stationers' are, or even what they're called!"

Sam sighed, the bubble of hope vanishing into the soapy smear of disillusion. He glanced down at the column of figures in front of him, and said simply and without any inflection,

"Legal Supplies, 22 Apothecary Row at the back of the tube station."

"Right, thanks, Mr. Coppock, back in a jiff."

Martin suddenly reminded Sam Coppock of the puppy he had had as a child. It used to bound around dementedly for half an hour at a time and then suddenly stop, wee on the carpet and fall into a deep, relaxed slumber. Sam glanced down at the carpet involuntarily and raised his eyebrows in relief.

Sam Coppock had not himself 'bounded' or 'fallen into' anything, least of all a relaxed slumber, for a long time. He was a calm and methodical man and was well aware that his place at the heart of the office was invaluable. Although he was a legal executive, rather than a solicitor, and was therefore a salaried employee, all the partners knew that he was due a deference and respect over and above that due to even their fellow partners. They might be the officers but Sam was the Regimental Sergeant Major who had saved their bacon on many occasions and knew where quite a few bodies were buried, figuratively speaking of course. To get anything done in the office, you needed to enlist Sam's support.

He was the master of delaying tactics and the sound of the breath being drawn in between his pursed lips had sounded the death knell of many a misguided partner's plans of modernisation or their intention to employ staff considered unsuitable by Sam.

One of his self-appointed tasks was to knock the rough and irritating edges off the occasional intake of articled clerks. They were the cheap labour imported under the pretext of training young hopefuls to be Solicitors of The Supreme Court and were mainly used as office boys, couriers, and repositories for all the routine and repetitive work. They were also frequently very handy as scapegoats for inactivity:

"I'm so sorry, Mrs. Pilkington, I asked my articled clerk to sort your Will out for you. Hasn't he been in touch? Oh really? Well, it couldn't be simpler, you should have had it by now. I'll get right on to it immediately! If you want a thing doing, as they say..."

The fact that the poor lad might never even have heard of the aforesaid Mrs. Pilkington was neither here nor there.

A client had been soothed with whatever excuse was to hand and the name of the firm remained unblemished.

Martin was standing at the counter of Legal Supplies in Apothecary Row. For over a hundred years, they had catered for the legal profession's office and stationery requirements which (it cannot be denied) were prodigious. With the advent of computers, the role of the Law Stationer would be diminished, but this was 1963 and the paperless society was in the distant future; the very distant future, as computers made very little difference to the consumption of paper, despite the intentions of those who invented them.

Back then, 'If it's worth saying, it's worth having a form to say it' seemed to be the joint maxim of both supplier and customer. It is rumoured that a waggish young solicitor once asked for an 'Application for Delivery of the Head and Entrails of the Condemned, (with supporting affidavit) under the High Treason, Rebellion and Dissent (Torture and Decapitation) Act 1411, as amended by the Licensing of Public Executions, Bear Baiting and Entertainment Act 1568' and was presented by the impassive assistant with two forms, one white and one buff, and the query "Nobleman or Commoner?"

Melanie Palmer was a pretty girl and understood perfectly the effect of pink angora sweaters on both her body and the young male heart rate. Men of all ages would try to assess the progress of the queue in the shop and loiter until they could join it at a point where they might be served by the delectable Melanie rather than grim Miss Pimlott or either of the bored and boring young male assistants, whose names were unknown to the majority of the predominantly male customer base. Melanie had worked at Legal Supplies for only a few months but she was a quick learner and knew how to put customers at their ease. She also knew, instinctively, like many of her sex who have been blessed with good looks, how to do precisely the opposite.

"Can I help you, sir?" she said automatically, closing the till as the previous customer staggered off with a box of printed Invoices (by far their most popular and profitable line).

Martin, in a careless and world weary tone which he earnestly, but vainly, hoped indicated that, for heaven's sake, this was an errand that he accomplished on a daily basis, said: "Oh, er – just a hundred Oral Agreement Forms please– oh and put them on Wolf, Rivers and Sherriff's Account, would you?"

Melanie looked at him carefully for a moment.

"Sorry, sir, what was that again?"

"A hundred Oral Agreement Forms please and put them on..."

"...Wolf Rivers and Sherriff's account, yes I heard that bit," she interrupted. "New articled clerk there are you?"

Martin had fondly imagined that his assured and confident manner would create the impression of a man accustomed to moving freely between the Old Bailey and the Chancery Court (whatever that was) and that he was on more than nodding terms with the Lord Chancellor. It came therefore as a grievous body blow to discover that he was quite so easily identifiable as the new kid on the block, but he persevered manfully nonetheless.

"Newish, yes," he confided. After all, he was well into his second hour!

He waited, while she nodded slowly gazing at him thoughtfully and took what seemed to Martin a disproportionately long time to assimilate this information.

He heard himself filling in the uncomfortable silence by adding,

"...been doing other things until quite recently."

Before he could mentally kick himself for this ridiculous attempt to impress her, she quickly responded, leaning forward over the counter and tilting her head to the right as if fascinated by this man of many parts in front of her,

"Oh yes? Sounds interesting. What sort of 'other things' would they be then?"

It was obviously out of the question to answer "A holiday job at 'Thrifty Print and Copy Shop' while waiting for my 'A' level results," so he replied vaguely, "Oh, a bit of 'this and that', you know."

"What about 'the other' then?"

Martin blushed furiously and then got angry with himself for betraying himself so completely by blushing.

"The, er ...other?"

"You know" she continued blinking innocently at him, "This, that and the other?"

"Oh, yes, of course, 'This that and the other,' yes, ha–ha yes, anyway now... er, about these forms..."

"Sorry what were they again?"

Her voice increased in volume just sufficiently to puncture the usual low hum of conversation in the shop. Assistants and customers alike became subtly aware that something interesting was taking place at the end of the counter. Martin too became conscious that something in the atmosphere had changed but couldn't put his finger on quite what it was.

"A hundred Oral Agreement forms please."

"Oh yes, that's right. Oral Agreement Forms! Silly me. That is what you said isn't it?"

She pronounced the words, it seemed to Martin, unnecessarily slowly and loudly. She continued,

"Do you want Statutory, Common Law or Section 42?"

Martin had a vague idea of the difference between Statute and Common Law but had no option but to ask, "Er, Section 42?"

Melanie examined her exquisite finger nails.

"Section 42 of the Miscellaneous Instruments Provisions 1897 provides for a Certification option in the event of non–reciprocal, fundamental variation." She looked up at him with a cheery smile "Is that what you're after?"

Martin cleared his throat. Fortunately, he had not noticed that everyone within hearing range was now intently studying any inanimate object to hand rather than catch anyone else's eye. The odd twitching shoulder was the only indication that Melanie's cabaret had an appreciative audience. Even Miss Pimlott's left eyebrow appeared to be experiencing some difficulty in maintaining its usual disapproving tilt.

Martin was desperate to extricate himself from this situation without losing face and seized on delaying tactics.

"Oh yes, Section Forty-*two*!" implying that he had thought she had said Section 41 or 43, with which he wasn't quite as familiar as good old section 42, with which he had a very close relationship, verging on intimacy and going back for many years.

"Well they're not for me, you see.... I'm picking them up for someone else, so I'd better go back and check, I suppose. Should have asked, of course. Don't want the office overflowing with forms that we've already got, do we? Got to think of the world timber stocks after all."

Melanie gave him a warm smile.

"That's right. The world timber stocks! I'm glad someone is thinking of them, I must say. See you later then!"

Martin was relieved on his return to the office, when he learnt from the receptionist that Sam Coppock had gone out on a completion and wouldn't be back for a while. He hadn't relished the thought of coming back a second time, empty handed from what had seemed an hour ago to be a fairly easy errand. On his tour of the office earlier in the day he had been taken into the senior secretaries' room, where Beryl, Eunice and Deirdre sat, with headphones on and fingers flying over the keyboards. He had been told that there was nothing about the running of the office, or indeed the minutiae of the business conducted by Wolf, Rivers and

Sheriff that was not known to those three ladies. As they were all outside the age category that Martin would have found intimidating (i.e. his own age category), he consulted the three wise typists.

He explained his problem. Beryl nodded gravely and told him that it wasn't her field – she was a probate and inheritance law secretary. Deirdre was more experienced in the contractual line.

While Martin explained again to Deirdre, Beryl had a nasty coughing fit and had to leave the room to get a glass of water. Deirdre consulted Eunice, who removed her headphones and listened as Deirdre explained that Martin had been sent on an errand by Sam Coppock to get Oral Agreement Forms and didn't know whether to get the Statutory, Common Law or Section 42 version.

"Oral Agreement Forms, but surely there's no..." began Eunice.

"No shortage of Common Law or Section 42 forms in the office, quite!" interrupted Deirdre, kicking Eunice under the table . "So Sam must have been after the Statutory ones. We get through a lot of them don't we, Eunice?"

Eunice seemed a little short of breath as she replied "Yes, it's bound to be the statutory ones – I remember noticing we were low on them when I was stocktaking last week."

As Martin left the room, he passed a watery eyed Beryl in the corridor.

"Sorted you out have they, dear?"

"Yes thanks, Beryl. It's the statutory ones apparently – thanks for all your help!"

"Like lambs to the slaughter...." thought Beryl watching him as he set briskly off down the stairs again.

Back at Legal Supplies, as Martin stepped up to the counter in front one of the bored young men, a voice from the other end of the counter called, "It's all right, Kevin, that's my customer – send him up here, would you?"

Martin felt a mixture of pleasure and pride that he should be memorable to this frankly rather desirable young lady but also feared that his inexperience in matters legal in particular (and matters social in general!) might not improve his chances of making a favourable impression.

"Apparently, it's the Statutory Oral Agreement Forms they want," he said, desperately trying to give the impression that the type of form was a trivial matter really, of minimal importance to him as he had more weighty concerns to occupy his mind and was only doing someone else a favour.

"Oh, that's really too bad." replied Melanie. "I'm so sorry, we're out of them. There's been a lot of demand lately, hasn't there Kevin?" she shouted across the shop to her colleague.

"What?" replied Kevin.

"There's been a lot of demand for Statutory Oral Agreement Forms, hasn't there? Wonder why?"

"People been making a lot of Statutory Oral Agreements, I suppose! Tell your customer they might have some at J.P.S.?" Kevin called back.

"J.P.S?" Martin asked.

"Jurisprudential Print Services in Bartergate; you can't miss them! Sorry we can't help you. I hope I'll be able to satisfy your requirements next time." Melanie flashed Martin her warmest smile and was gratified to see a pink flush suffuse his cheeks. He breathed deeply in through his nose so that he could remember that scent that she wore – a heady, musky mixture which worked its magic so well that, for years to come, the same pungent combination of that aroma combined with blonde hair, blue eyes and pink angora would render him insensible to reason.

Martin arrived at J.P.S. a little while later in confident mood. Here there would be no problem. He was on top of the situation and would shortly accomplish his errand.

It was a dingy shop with one youth behind the counter chatting to an older man in a boiler suit who was draining an old fashioned iron radiator, mounted on the wall beneath a large calendar depicting a range of mind numbingly dull paper clips, ink pads and rubber bands.

"Excuse me?"

"Yeah?" replied the youth, a little irritated at being interrupted while giving his riveting account to the plumber of how he had triumphed in a darts competition the previous evening, by getting treble 18, 20 and double top.

"Do you have any Oral Agreement Forms? Statutory rather than Common Law or section 42," he added to indicate that he knew what he was talking about.

"Dunno. I'll go and ask."

As he ambled gently into the darker recesses of the shop, the older man looked up from his radiator and said,

"In my line, it's left handed spanners".

"I'm sorry?"

"Someone's winding you up, son. Every new apprentice in my line always got sent on some stupid errand on his first day, like getting a left handed spanner, so wherever you went everyone knew you were wet behind the ears and sent you off on another wild goose chase. Just a bit of fun I suppose, but I remember feeling a right prat because I didn't tumble it for hours!"

The penny still didn't drop. Martin looked at him with a furrowed brow and while his brain was grappling with the possibility that he was being taken for a fool, he temporised with a confused "Sorry, what? I don't understand. You mean..."

"Look, if you had a form for it, it wouldn't be an *oral* agreement would it? I might be wrong but that's what I'd say anyway, but you probably know what you're on about. I don't know much about the law, apart from the fact that when you need it, it costs you an arm and a leg!"

During this conversation, the shop assistant had been briefed fully by his boss on how to continue the joke at Martin's expense and was disappointed to discover on his return that the butt of his intended laborious humour had fled.

Later that day, when Sam Coppock returned from his completion, he found on his desk a pile of 100 crisp new forms.

Sam read the heading: "Statutory Oral Agreement Form." He raised an eyebrow and read on with interest.

"This Agreement is intended for use when the terms of an Oral Agreement fall outside the Provision of the Contractual Clauses (Verbal Variations) Orders and in the event of a failure of the non-specific clarification procedures identified by a Winding Up Order as amended by the Pursuit of Wild Geese Act 1923.
This Agreement is made ..."

To the surprise of one of the partners who had just entered the office, Sam started to laugh – a rare event.

Perhaps this one might prove to be interesting, he thought.

Who would have imagined it?

Martin had paid a visit to his friends and former colleagues at the Thrifty Print and Copy Shop where he had spent a profitable if unexciting summer. A half an hour on their type setter and copying machine had equipped him with the means of turning the events of his first day at Wolf, Rivers and Sheriff to his advantage.

Later that evening, Martin's father asked how the first day had gone and was somewhat nonplussed when he received the reply,

"Oh very well really, they were having a little problem with the drafting of a particular legal document. You wouldn't understand – it's rather complicated. Anyway I managed to sort it out for them and came up with something that fitted the bill alright. They seemed almost embarrassed about it. Can't imagine why!"

If You Could Read My Mind

"For heaven's sake, can't you do anything right? Oh. I give up!"

Alex East snatched the un-posted letters up from the shelf by the door and hurled them back down again in rage.

His wife Elizabeth protested.

"But I told you not to ask me to post them. I can't help it – I just have a terrible memory for things like that, however hard I try to remember. I really do try…"

It was too late. The sound of his feet thumping angrily up the stairs echoed with the threat of another evening of criticism and continuous sighs as he affected a heavy handed "tolerance", which was slowly eroding what little self-confidence she had.

His voice thundered from above.

"And turn that bloody awful music off. How many times do I have to tell you – I can't stand Barbra Streisand! In fact I can't stand any of your abysmal choice in music. Turn it off for God's sake!"

She went across to the CD player and pressed the off switch before returning to the kitchen to prepare the evening meal.

The night before had been even worse. They had entertained the Wardles. Richard and Tish Wardle were bright, sophisticated, witty and charming. And despite the fact that they were very pleasant people, there was an inescapable whiff of smugness about them. But then no-one's perfect!

They had met Alex at Cambridge, where Richard was President of the Union and Tish was a bright young thing, who was at every party and still managed to get a good second. She was now an effortless hostess who had entertained Alex and Elizabeth on many occasions, mainly these days because they liked Elizabeth, though she could never quite believe that these "glitterati" could view her as anything other than the Secondary Modern girl from Northampton that she was.

Alex, though he had never shone particularly at Cambridge, had proved to be the most successful of them in many ways. As the lawyer for Baxter Communication Industries, he had steered the Company through the tricky waters of a recent take–over battle and been well rewarded when Baxters came out on top. Alex was untroubled by any concern beyond that which might significantly enhance his own progress onwards and upwards and the interests of Baxter Industries, insofar as those two aims did not conflict, which, thus far, at least, they had not.

Richard however had, in Alex's eyes, squandered his education and qualifications by opting to take over the family publishing business, when his father died. It was a small scale, well respected and privately owned company, which published mainly poetry and scholastic works of art history and criticism. A modest living was all that could be garnered from W. R. Wardle & Co.

Tish, on the other hand, perplexed Alex even more. Despite her good brain, she was teaching children with "Special Educational Needs", albeit at a Church Middle School in the leafy suburbs.

"Why, in God's name, do you want to go and waste your damned good education on thickies?" Alex once demanded, with a characteristic lack of charm or understanding. "Let the Secondary Moderns and Comprehensives look after them (no offence Lizzie!) – and use your brain. If I'd got your degree, you wouldn't see me for dust. I certainly wouldn't be wasting my time on kids who are never going to amount to anything or contribute a bloody thing to society."

"Oh, Alex!" Tish had admonished. "Don't pretend to be such a ghastly boor. It doesn't suit you. How do you put up with him, Lizzie?"

Before Elizabeth could answer, Alex leaped in "Oho, she knows when she's on to a good thing. Don't you worry. Am I right or am I right, Lizzie? I'm right! Now how's about getting that coffee, old girl, Richard and Tish have almost got their tongues hanging out, for heaven's sake!"

Unable to bear anything that might be termed "a scene", Elizabeth had complied with Alex's request, which had been made in the weary tone of a schoolmaster who was explaining a basic instruction for the umpteenth time. She had never got used to his apparent distaste for everything about her, but neither had she ever found a way of countering it or dealing with it. Well-meaning friends had offered many solutions ranging from divorce to playing him at his own game, but none of the solutions were acceptable to her.

She found it hard to reconcile his current attitude and persona with the memory of his insistent and overwhelming courtship of her. He had spent several days in a Private Hospital, after having had an operation on his knee to correct an old school sporting injury. Elizabeth had been his nurse. She was pretty, kind and cheerful. He was still smarting from the recent split with his long time live–in lover, Natalie. Elizabeth was as different as it was possible to be from the power–dressing, challenging and controversial Natalie. Elizabeth was a blonde, Natalie was a brunette. Natalie was an astute business woman, with degrees in History and Sociology, could cook superbly, (when she chose to) and rode to hounds with the Hunt, of which her god–father was joint Master. She was a social asset and could easily dominate any dinner table with her quick wit and acerbic tongue. She was totally in control of herself and her life – from which she expected a lot, and which was probably why she eventually tired of Alex.

Elizabeth on the other hand was just... well... *nice*. She felt no desire to dominate anyone or even compete with them. She wanted children. But Alex had had a vasectomy at Natalie's insistence – a fact which he had not shared with her until some time after they were married. It was a bitter blow to Elizabeth who had succumbed to the common fallacy that children might improve their already tottering relationship. It was an even harsher blow to them both, therefore, when they read in the Daily Telegraph that Natalie had had twins by the TV producer whom she had subsequently married. Natalie and Quentin and their sons were on the cover of every colour magazine for weeks and Alex became, if that were remotely possible, even more demanding and impossible to satisfy.

Whereas until then Natalie had been an unspoken wedge between them, he no longer felt the need to keep his feelings about her to himself. His desire to hurt someone who could not fight back focused, as always, on the one who loved him the most and had done the least to harm him. Now he openly compared her to the paragon that was Natalie.

If she baked a cake, Natalie had baked a better one. In love–making, why couldn't she be more spontaneous – a little more adventurous? (Natalie had been a tiger, apparently). Why didn't she have some other interests outside the home and the ruddy animals? (Elizabeth's soft heart had led her to provide sanctuary for two farm cats, a mongrel and an elderly donkey which was housed in the neighbouring field of an affable farmer.)

Why, oh why, was she always so apologetic? For four years now friends had witnessed the steady erosion of Elizabeth's self–confidence. Her cheerful, bright demeanour had gradually faded to be replaced by a desperation to please when she was in his presence. Only when he had been away for a few days on a business trip did the old Elizabeth, with a ready smile for everyone, begin to re–appear. Even Alex's friends, like Tish and Richard began to feel protective towards her and do their best to protect her from his worst excesses of scorn and criticism.

Last night had been the culmination of a period of steadily intensifying sniping. Elizabeth had prepared dinner, taking great pains to ensure that there would be nothing for Alex to fault. She had spent hours poring over her Elizabeth David and trekked half way across the county to get the best ingredients. Knowing that Alex would be late and would bark at her for failing to open the correct wine, she had taken the precaution of phoning his wine merchant for advice. The Chateau Lynch Bages was un-corked, the Chateau Bauduc Les Trois Hectares was chilled. She had remembered Richard's allergy to shell–fish. Surely, please, nothing could go wrong tonight?

Alex was, as she had expected, late. He exploded into what he insisted on calling "the drawing room", cursing his work colleagues for their inability to grasp a simple concept and making him go over old ground a thousand times at their afternoon meeting. They were all, of course, morons.

"Then, of course," he continued, "the train was crowded with malodorous bank clerks and spotty secretaries not to mention some doddering old fool who felt entitled to berate me for talking on my telephone! For God's sake, do these people have no concept of the pressures one is under in the business world these days? There just aren't enough hours in the day, without people with bugger all to do whingeing about those of us who have to get on with keeping the country afloat while they read their papers! And then my ruddy car was blocked in for simply ages by some bloody silly woman who couldn't get out of a space that a sodding pantechnicon could have done wheelies in, for God's sake. Anyway..."

He paused for breath and gazed at his audience.

"Has Lizzie given you a drink chaps? Ah yes, I see she has – only Lizzie could have put a slice of lemon in a Campari! Shall I get you another one, Tish?" Before Tish could demur, he swept the glass out of her hand and disappeared into the kitchen, followed by Lizzie apologising to Tish over her shoulder.

"I'm sorry, Alex – I was thinking "orange" but sliced a lemon. It's been hectic here today. You didn't tell me the man was coming to put the new power points in the study. I had no electricity for two hours and then the hospital rang with the results of my..." Before she could continue, "Not now please, darling!" he barked, "It may have escaped your notice that our guests are on their own, which of course wouldn't have happened if you had been paying attention to what you were doing and not dreaming, as usual! I don't know what gets into you sometimes, I really don't! And what are you wearing those ridiculous clothes for? You're like a hippy who's been to a jumble sale, for God's sake – it's embarrassing!"

Elizabeth fought back the tears and slowly returned to join Richard and Tish who had clearly heard the exchange in the kitchen and were anxious to pour some oil of human kindness on the troubled waters. "You are a blithering idiot sometimes, Alex," said Tish, putting an arm around Elizabeth's shoulders, "I was perfectly happy with my drink and Elizabeth has been entertaining us beautifully. Have an olive and calm down. Now what were you telling us about the new people down the road..."

The rest of the evening passed relatively uneventfully apart from Alex's usual tendency to dominate every conversation and deflect it back in his own direction.

As they said their goodbyes at the front door, Tish gave Elizabeth a hug and whispered in her ear, "I'll give you a call tomorrow; we'll have a lunch – just the two of us," she added quickly in case Elizabeth thought she might be suggesting another opportunity for her husband to patronise and humiliate her publicly. "Don't let him get at you darling. I don't know what's wrong with him these days." She kissed her on the cheek and followed her husband who was holding the car door open for her. Elizabeth couldn't help remembering that Alex used to do that for her. But the courtesy had stopped very soon after they got married.

As she turned to re-enter the house, she saw her husband climbing the stairs. He threw over his shoulder,

"I'm off to have a long soak, Lizzie, and watch a bit of telly in bed. I'm completely knackered. I've had a hell of a day and I need to be fresh for tomorrow. I'm playing squash with Mack before I go to work and he nearly beat me last week. Can't have that, can we? Try not to drop anything when you're clearing up, there's a good girl."

She watched him turn the corner onto the landing and heard the sound of the water pouring into his bath. Despite her best efforts, tears of frustration and loneliness puddled in her eyes and slowly overflowed down her pale cheeks. She lowered her head and walked slowly into the back kitchen to let Barney out. Alex wasn't fond of animals at the best of times and insisted that they were not allowed in reception rooms when they had guests. So Barney, who adored Elizabeth and would not be more than a bone's length away from her at any time if he had his way, came tumbling out exuding bonhomie and affection, which Elizabeth sorely needed at that point. She knelt down and hugged him, scratching him vigorously behind his ears, an activity that sent him into his usual canine state of rigid bliss. When she stopped and stood up, he followed her backwards and forwards as she cleared the dining table and set about restoring the place to its usual immaculate state. Any blemish would attract a sour comment from Alex in the morning, along the lines of "You haven't even put the decanter back in the right place. Do I have to do everything myself?" – ignoring the fact that he actually did nothing in the house at all, well – other than carp, complain and criticise.

So it was no surprise the following morning when the one thing she hadn't done was seized upon by the Inquisitor General that was her husband: Why, oh why, had she forgotten his letters? It never occurred to her to question why he hadn't taken them with him in the morning. There was a post box only forty yards away from the car park by the station. He could easily have taken them himself. It was almost as if he wanted to prove to himself that he had a good reason to find fault with her, rather than face up to the fact that he was a bully plain and simple. As he left he told her, with heavy sarcasm dripping from every syllable, that if she could spare some in her busy day doing God knows what to post his letters he would be very grateful. And he was borrowing her car for the day as his was being collected that morning to have a new entertainment system installed by the dealers as the present one was woeful and not the spec he had expected when he had bought the ruddy thing off them last month.

He had then snatched her car keys up from the kitchen and stood staring at her for a moment as she gazed mutely at him

"I just wish you could stop letting me down all the time Lizzie! I don't ask much do I? Just a well-run home and the occasional decent meal for our friends. All that emotional stuff last night! For heaven's sake! I really don't care to have my friends telling me how unhappy you are, as if I am somehow to blame, when you and I both know that you are the architect of your own misfortune. I don't know what you've been saying to them, but I don't take kindly to you laying your failures at my door!"

He then turned and headed for the door. "And don't forget the letters... for God's sake!"

She followed him and stood in the open doorway watching his retreating figure. He turned when he reached her car and shouted back to her 'I'm going to have dinner at the club tonight and stay there. If you can't be bothered to do a simple thing for me, I see no reason why I should have to listen to your feeble excuses for the rest of the evening. For heaven's sake woman, shape up or ship out!" That was one of his favourite expressions. All his staff had heard him use it at some time or another and despite their desire to respond with derision at such a hackneyed Americanism, they bit their lips because Alex had the power to hire and fire and loved exercising that power.

As she returned to the house and shut the door quietly behind her, Barney came padding out from the utility room where he had learned it was safer to stay until he was alone in the house with Elizabeth. He nuzzled her hand and she crouched down to hug him.

'I'll just go and post his letters Barney dear, and then we'll go and have a lovely walk in the woods' she whispered into his neck and, as if understanding her completely, he trotted back to curl up in his bed by the washing machine.

She had intended to walk down to the nearest post–box in the village, but as Alex's car had not yet been collected, she thought she would use it to save time and collecting his keys from the hall stand went outside and got into his car. She placed the letters on the dashboard and drove off.

When she reached the little village post office, her braking had caused the letters to slide off the dashboard onto the floor under the driver's seat.

So when she got out of the car, she reached under the seat to retrieve them and found that there were more letters there than she had expected. In addition to the ones she had been ordered to post, there were several envelopes addressed to Alex at a post–box number, which had clearly been opened and returned to their envelopes. Although it was not in her nature, after she popped the new letters into the box, she sat in the car for a few moments reading the letters that Alex had put under the seat of his car.

Her world was already not a pleasant or comfortable one. Within a few seconds it became infinitely worse. The letters were from a woman called Katya. It appeared that Alex and Katya had been having an affair for some time and in the letters she was advising him on the most effective method of stashing away his assets in a way that would minimise the financial effect of his divorcing Elizabeth in the very near future. Katya it appeared was not only his mistress but a successful divorce lawyer in London. The letters were recent but the affair, from what she could discern from the tone and content of the letters, was long standing.

Elizabeth drove slowly home, parked the car and placed the letters back where she had found them.

As she walked through the woods with Barney a few minutes later, her brain was churning with chaotic tumbling thoughts. Emotions whirled around and confused her. She was shocked and yet not surprised, stunned and yet relieved in a perverse way, miserable and yet saw a glimmer of a possibility that her life might just be moving in a new direction that would eventually be an improvement on the living desperation of her day to day life at the moment.

By the time she had returned home and placed Barney's bowl of food on the floor, she had reached a decision. She was going to confront Alex and she was not going to allow him to browbeat her for one more moment. She now was in a position to stand up for herself she had decided and she was going to do so.

Her Road to Damascus moment was rudely interrupted by the ringing of the front doorbell that was to bring her the news that was to lurch her life into yet another unexpected direction.

It was the Police.

There had been an accident.

Alex, she was told, had been seriously injured while trying to overtake a farm tractor on a country lane and was in hospital. They could take her to him, but he was unconscious and, they warned her, liable to remain so for some time.

As it turned out, they were right.

When he did eventually return to full consciousness several months later, he was paralysed, able to move only his eyes and that only minimally. The consultants were only persuaded that he could be returned to be cared for in his home by the fact that his wife was a trained nurse who had satisfied them that she was able to supervise his ongoing care quite efficiently at their home.

During his months in intensive care, Elizabeth had contacted Katya and informed her that she knew of both their affair and their plans and indicated that she was perfectly happy to surrender her husband to the obviously more attractive arms of his inamorata. Their new life together could start now and she would not stand in their way; and she was sure that Katya's substantial income as a successful lawyer would be more than adequate to add to whatever insurance monies were allocated to Alex's future care. To no one's surprise Katya had other plans and did not even pay a visit to the hospital before or after Alex emerged from his coma.

Elizabeth also set about unravelling Alex's complicated financial affairs and found that Katya's advice had not (at the point of the accident) even begun to be implemented and that she and Alex were very well set up for the rest of their lives.

Gradually all Alex's erstwhile big buddies faded into the background and disappeared although Tish and Richard still came round occasionally for a meal, often bringing a take-away to ease the burden on Elizabeth.

They would sit around the table in the same large room as Alex lay supine and unmoving and, convinced by Elizabeth that he 'loved the sound of people enjoying themselves', they would drink and laugh together into the wee small hours, with 'his favourite music' Barbra Streisand, playing in the background.

She had acquired several new companions to keep her company during the long days spent caring for her husband. A Jack Russell terrier and spaniel had joined Barney the amiable cross breed and roamed the house at will. And a pair of black and white farm cats had joined them too. One of them, Monty, loved to lie on Alex's bed by his side and Elizabeth told everyone that Alex loved cats and she could tell that when Monty was around he felt calmer. She knew him so well, she would insist, that even in his current state of inability to communicate she knew what eased the undoubted tedium of his long days trapped in an unresponsive body.

She told everyone too that when they had met, he loved the fact that she was wearing 'hippy' clothes long after everyone else was wearing them – and that it made him think of the fun times of his youth – so even though she personally didn't care for them, she wore them for him in the hope that it might spark some sort of response one day.

Before Tish and Richard left after a long evening, during which they had played 'Snap' loudly and sang songs from the musicals they gathered round the bed to say goodbye to Alex. As they each gave the unresponsive form their cheery message of encouragement, that Alex would have found mawkish and intolerable before the accident, she smiled fondly down at the still form of the man she had married for better or for worse.

"Do think he understand us?" whispered Tish as they walked towards the door.

"Oh yes I am sure he does," replied Elizabeth, as she turned up the volume of the CD player and the strains of Barbra plaintively singing 'If you could read my mind' filled the house. "His neurosurgeon says that all the evidence points to the fact that he understands everything that is going on, but he just cannot respond in any meaningful way, poor dear."

She returned to the bedside of her husband and looked down at him thoughtfully, as she stroked Monty's neck. The cat was curled up against Alex's chest and arched and purred with pleasure as her hands gently tickled his neck. She joined in with Barbra, singing, "But the feelin's gone And I just can't get it back."

Hamlet's Ghost

The Arts Festival had seemed a good idea at the time.

Alderman Adrian Clegg–Potter was a man with a strong sense of history and an even stronger sense of his own importance in the scheme of things. The fact that he had a hyphenated surname said it all as far he was concerned. He neither knew nor cared that that the double barrel was solely the result of the refusal of a wealthy Clegg ancestor to relinquish her surname when she married a compliant Potter ancestor who cared a lot more about his impending life on easy street than he did about maintaining the primacy of his ancestors' surname. History mattered not a whit to Adrian; he wanted the name of Clegg–Potter, his name, to figure largely in the annals of Godminster for generations to come – but, more importantly, he wanted it to figure in great big capital letters *now*. He wanted the respect and admiration that was due to great benefactors and servants of the community to be accorded to him while he was still around to bask in it and to benefit from it. Reflected glory was not for him; he wanted the real, unadulterated, right–there–in–the–spotlight thing. The kind of glory that comes with being a pillar of the community; and indeed many people thought of him as a pillar – or a word very similar to that anyway. The only way to ensure that, for instance, the new community leisure centre bore his name when it was completed in three years' time was to do something so high profile that no other name was possible. He was therefore not entirely altruistic when he informed everyone that mattered in the community that he wanted the town to celebrate the bicentenary of Godminster's Charter in style. And if the only way for that to happen meant that he, the chairman of the council, a former mayor and current chairman of the town's magistrates, had to sacrifice even more of his valuable free time in the interests of the citizens of Godminster, then so be it. He was equal to the task and ready to shoulder the burden of masterminding the whole bicentennial celebration himself. His willing colleagues bowed with alacrity to his will and heaved a huge sigh relief. They all knew that he was not a willing delegator of the big decisions and therefore he would carry the can if it went wrong and they could all nod wisely and escape the flak after the event.

An apocryphal link between the town and Shakespeare had persuaded the Alderman and, more importantly his wife, Eileen, that the work of the world's greatest playwright should feature heavily in the bicentennial festival. Eileen Clegg–Potter was the dominant force in the Godminster and Middlethorp Players Society (GAMPS) and saw the event as an opportunity to display her prodigious wares to a wider audience than normally attended the Society's performances in the Battersby Memorial Hall when it wasn't needed by the Young Mothers' Group, Scouts and Women's Institute.

According to local Guide Books, Shakespeare had received the inspiration for his second play - *The Comedy of Errors* - from a misunderstanding one night resulting from a foolish adventure involving the twin seventeen year old daughters of mine host at Godminster's Coaching Inn. The present name of the inn – "The Maid and Trollop" – survives as a salutary lesson to any future itinerant bards, or indeed those modern day commercial travellers so celebrated in unlikely and lascivious anecdote, of the inadvisability of accepting advice from apparently simple local yokels, when inebriated and far from home. Had Will not managed a swift, if undignified, exit from the hostelry via the route normally used for emptying the chamber pots, then his prodigious output may well have been restricted to *Love's Labours Lost*, an irony which probably would have escaped him and probably future generations in that unfortunate eventuality.

At any rate, Alderman Clegg–Potter was highly motivated by the desire to keep Eileen happy – and, more importantly, busy – for the next several months. A happy Eileen Clegg–Potter was an Eileen Clegg–Potter who was not on his case twenty four hours a day. And a busy Eileen Clegg–Potter meant that she didn't have time to ask him what he's been doing minute by minute during those twenty four hours. Eileen's immersion in the dramatic element of the festival for weeks on end would therefore give him the opportunity to spend more time discussing matters of a confidential nature with Mrs. Barraclough, the local councillor who held the portfolio for Younger and Older People – a portfolio which many found baffling, both in its composition of what might seem to be polar opposites and its exclusion of all the other people who arguably contributed the lions' share of the council tax. Anyway, those considerations aside, Alderman Clegg–Potter's discussions with this doughty representative of some of the people some of the time necessitated the absolute certainty of quiet seclusion and freedom from interruption or subsequent interrogation by anyone at all really, but principally the equally doughty Eileen.

He therefore used all his considerable (and very visible) weight and influence locally to ensure widespread support for the Festival. He was able to persuade his colleagues from the Chamber of Commerce to fund the project by the simple expedient of letting it be known that his Property Company would be significantly less likely to increase commercial letting rates to local businesses if he was heavily involved with organising the Arts Festival – as he would be unable to conduct a review of the existing rents, which were, of course, demonstrably well below current market levels. Sponsorship came flooding in, and even local councillors, whose proletarian roots made them deeply suspicious of anything remotely "arty–farty", dropped their objections to the scheme when convinced it wouldn't involve any loss of income for their pet community projects (like Roller Skating facilities for the over eighties and free corporal punishment for masochists).

Eventually, when everything had been agreed and scheduled, Eileen Clegg–Potter got round to reading *The Comedy of Errors*. For all her faults, she was not a stupid woman when it came to recognising and seizing opportunities for her own aggrandisement. She had after all married Adrian Clegg–Potter, a course of action which many less ambitious women may have considered a price too high to pay for even the level of social and financial benefits he was able to offer, but Eileen had no such compunctions and sensed immediately that Cleggy would be easily managed. And by her own standards she was right. This then was the woman who struggled through the play and immediately realised that there was no natural starring role that would offer her the opportunity to display her undoubted ability to talk much more loudly than anyone else. She was blessed with a stentorian instrument that would be envied by town criers the world over. Indeed, it was a source of great regret to the majority of her past audiences that along with her other manifold shortcomings as an actress she did not suffer from the one deficiency that might serve to make all the others tolerable: inaudibility.

Once she had discovered the dismal failure of the Swan of Avon to provide a role for her in his *Comedy of Errors*, it took her no time at all to convince her husband that, despite the celebrated connection of the town with that particular play, the occasion of Godminster's bi–centenary would be much better celebrated by a performance of Shakespeare's most famous and therefore obviously, by definition, best play. *Hamlet* then it was to be.

After a brief dalliance with the beguiling notion of playing Ophelia, Eileen Clegg–Potter announced to an unsurprised world that the casting committee had been kind enough to decree that she should play Gertrude, Queen of Denmark and Mother to the eponymous Hamlet. It was not, it should be understood, any awareness of the singular inappropriateness of a middle–aged woman of ample frame and booming voice playing the "nymph in her orisons" that dictated her final choice of role. It was merely that Gertrude had more lines and died dramatically from poison on stage, unlike Ophelia, whose untimely demise occurred offstage and was reported by others some considerable time before the climactic end of the play.

A complication had arisen when it was discovered that the anniversary of the Charter fell in the same week in early January that the Local Education Committee had booked the Godminster Assembly Rooms for the joint Primary and Middle Schools' performance of Jack and the Beanstalk, which the children of all the schools in the Borough had been rehearsing for four months. Alderman Clegg–Potter had not become the dominant force that he was in local politics without being very aware of the very real political danger of alienating the doting parents of cute little infants. However, some swift manoeuvrings and promises of preferment and advancement had convinced the officers of the Education Department to offer the schools the adjoining facilities of the Mayor's Hall, which whilst smaller, "had a better acoustic so that the little lambs could be heard properly and appreciated by their adoring families."

The other factor that contributed so spectacularly to the destruction of the grand opening night was the decision to record the voice of the ghost of Hamlet's father on tape. The customary shortage of willing male actors encouraged the director to make a virtue of necessity and take the opportunity to work some technical wizardry on the sound system to give a sonorous and ethereal quality to the disembodied and pre-recorded voice of the ghost of the troubled dead king. It was a well-intentioned error that in more capable hands and with the blessing of the fates might have been very effective.

On the opening night dignitaries had been dredged up from far and wide. County Sheriffs, Mayors of neighbouring boroughs, MPs and even the Under-Secretary of State from the Heritage Ministry had been coerced or cajoled to attend the production.

When it had been discovered at the early stages of rehearsal that the play had a potential running time of over four hours, it had been drastically edited in order to achieve the more acceptable length of one and a half hours. This had been achieved, not unsurprisingly to those who knew her, without any significant diminution in the role of Gertrude and involved the wholesale jettisoning of subsidiary roles like Rosencrantz and Guildenstern, Marcellus and Bernardo and the demotion of Polonius, Laertes and Claudius to what were, in the event, minor supporting roles. Hamlet lost several of his soliloquies and only retained "To be or not to be" when it was very tentatively pointed out by the director (who knew his place in the scheme of things), that, whilst he absolutely agreed with Eileen Clegg-Potter that it slowed the action down, nonetheless the audience might just expect to hear Shakespeare's most famous lines in Shakespeare's most famous play and feel cheated were they to be excised. He reinforced the unassailable logic of that contention with the inspired suggestion that it would give Mrs. Clegg-Potter even more time to change into something majestic and wonderful to sit and watch the players do their (much truncated) thing.

As a result of Hamlet's death of a thousand cuts long before his demise at the hands of Laertes, the play opened with Shakespeare's fourth scene, where Hamlet meets the ghost of his late father.

On the opening night of Hamlet, in the adjacent Mayor's Hall, they were having their own problems. The two boys who had been originally cast to play the role of Daisy the Cow had succumbed to food poisoning, after foolishly consuming large quantities of some three day old canapés which had been left on a tray in the kitchen adjoining the Mayor's parlour, where they had been obliged to wait before making their grand entrance on the first night of Jack and the Beanstalk the previous evening. Two older boys, Gavin and Terry, from the Comprehensive School had been drafted in at very short notice to take their places. They had been given very strict instructions.

They were to wait in the kitchen area until the internal telephone rang three times and then stopped. They had to be in position a considerable time before the allotted moment for their appearance, as there was no means of accessing the kitchen without being seen by the audience who were admitted half an hour before the play began. The producer of the pantomime explained to them that while they were waiting they were, under no circumstances, to eat anything that they might find there. They were told of the unfortunate fate that had befallen the previous inhabitants of the cow costume and promised a slap up meal of their choice after the show was over. They were told to sit there with their cow 'legs' on ready and when the phone rang three times, they should get into the rest of the costume, make their way to the end of the corridor and wait by the double set of doors marked "No Entry – Staff Only". The stage manager, Geoff, would be waiting there to guide them through the doors and on to the set in time for their cue. Once on stage they should go to the centre back of the stage and do "general cow-like things" until Jack came up to them and led them off. Under no circumstances were they to leave the stage before then, on pain of death! Jack's Mum and the Giant's henchman would be pulling them to and fro in the interim from time to time, but it was impressed upon them that they should not allow themselves to be led off the stage or move a muscle until Jack's line, and did they remember what that line was?

Gavin and Terry reassured them for the umpteenth time that they fully understood their instructions and knew their cue line perfectly.

"Yeah, okay, we'll stay there once we're led on by Geoff and we won't leave the stage until Jack says 'Come on Daisy let's do as we're told, you're off to the market, there to be sold'. It's okay we'll remember, no problemo."

When the phone eventually rang, the boys were in the middle of a competition to see who could build the highest tower out of the cups and saucers that were stacked in trays in the Mayor's Parlour kitchen. They hadn't, at that point, even tried the costume on, under the (correct, as it turned out) impression that they were not required for some considerable time yet. They were competing in their tower building enterprise on the basis that the loser should occupy the rear end of Daisy, each threatening the other with the possible dire consequences of "that Vindaloo I had last night" to the accompaniment of much mirth and vocal demonstrations of the hideous consequences of finding themselves crouched, cheek to a different kind of cheek, at the less friendly end of the cow. Although the phone call was, in fact, only intended to check that they were alright and tell them that their bovine services would be required in about twenty five minutes, they failed to remember that their cue was three rings only, panicked and rushed headlong from the room fighting to be the first to get into the front end of the cow. By the time they reached the wrong end of the corridor that ran alongside the Mayor's Parlour, they had finally succeeded in cramming themselves uncomfortably into the costume. Gavin was at the front, having been threatened with savage retribution should his digestive tract produce any of the unsociable effects promised earlier on Terry's ability to breathe the already stale air within the costume.

The cow was robustly made, but for smaller occupants. A lethal combination. Having pulled the head down over his own, Gavin found that it was impossibly constricting. He could see very little out of the peephole through Daisy's mouth, which was not only designed for a Cyclops, but it was designed for a Cyclops that was considerably smaller than himself. He could just about contrive to see his own feet, now encased in sturdy brown and white cloven hooves. He found the ring pulls that he had been told controlled the cow's luxurious eyelashes and Terry, hanging on to the framework inside the cow, found the string that operated the cow's tail. They waited for Geoff, the stage manager, to come and collect them and guide them to the point in the wings from which they could make their entrance on to the stage. After a few minutes only, they made another fatal mistake, one arguably that had even more unwanted effects than that made by William Shakespeare when he visited, all those years ago, the coaching inn that was a mere hundred yards from the spot on which they now stood. They had earlier noticed that Geoff, the stage manager, had seemed distracted and somewhat vague when the producer had called him over to introduce him to the new occupants of the cow and discuss the procedure for their first entrance. There was good reason for this. The Health and Safety officer for the local council, in whose building they were performing, had just a moment earlier decreed that the beanstalk did not comply with the relevant regulations re working at heights and could not be persuaded that the fact that no–one actually climbed it should make some difference, surely? It had taken the late intervention of the chief executive of the council, (whose son was giving his 'Silly Billy' in the panto) to convince the jobsworth officer to allow the show to go ahead. Gavin and Terry had interpreted Geoff's distracted demeanour as indicating that he had not acknowledged his role in ensuring their safe arrival on the stage and decided, for perhaps the first (and hopefully last) occasion in their lives to use their initiative. Later, as is traditional in the theatre when things go awry, each was to blame the other for the consequences of their fateful decision. But, fearing that they were late for their appointed entrance, they moved purposefully and erratically through the swing doors.

Meanwhile, back in the Assembly Rooms, the curtain had risen on the battlements of Elsinore. The designer had taken the opportunity offered by the staging of this prestigious production to give vent to the creative excesses that can often occur when hitherto small players in the great drama of life get the opportunity to step out from the shadows and into the limelight. He grandly announced that he wanted to 'get away from the predictable traditional and naturalistic setting demanded by the play' and had created a set which drew on what he saw to be the underlying message of the play, which had never before (in his opinion) been thoroughly explored. It did not occur to the production team – which mainly comprised Mrs. Clegg–Potter – that it might be a mistake to so summarily dismiss the artistic endeavours of the Royal Shakespeare Company and other great theatres over several hundred years. Indeed, to the contrary, the designer, Hobson Tattersall, a graduate of the Godminster College of Design and Technology, was Mrs. Clegg–Potter's protégé, a role he had won by the simple expedient of regularly and loudly agreeing with everything she said and convincing her that she had come up with all the ideas that he carefully fed to her over a sweet martini in the Maid and Trollop after planning meetings. It should be understood that the sweet Martini was Hobson's choice;

Mrs. Clegg–Potter was a 'stout' person in every sense of that word.

Hobson's vision, now widely understood to be Mrs. Clegg–Potter's vision, involved the construction of separate acting areas on raised daises. These daises were not interconnected and made any physical contact between the participants well-nigh impossible. The intention of this disconnected staging was apparently to convey the 'intrinsic separation of all human beings'. At the back of the acting area there were contorted and disjointed fragments of blown–up cut–outs depicting great thinkers like Sophocles, Einstein, Descartes, Nietzsche and Freud, none of whom were easily identifiable by anyone other than Hobson himself who was, at the moment the lights came up, sulking in The Maid and Trollop because his voluminous and learned tedious explanatory notes had been left out of the souvenir programme in order to accommodate (prophetically as it turned out) a late full page advert by a company providing a comprehensive county–wide artificial insemination service for cattle. Mercifully, the printers had persuaded the advertisers that it might be wise to modify their original strap line – 'A Load of Bull' – a line that was later to be used with great glee, however, by the reviewer of the show for the local paper, who had been reluctantly press–ganged by the editor into forsaking his customary role as sports' reporter for the night of the great celebration.

Dominating the jagged representations of 'the great thinkers', in the centre of the back–cloth, was suspended a great polystyrene recreation of the prancing Godminster Bull, which had been the symbol of the town since the date of its charter two hundred years ago, when the cattle market was the town's main source of income. Hobson had instructed the stage management team to decorate the bull's horns with garlands of rosemary, pansies, fennel, columbines, rue and violets, the flowers and herbs mentioned by the deranged Ophelia in Act IV of the play.

Sadly January and Northern England are neither the ideal time nor place to source these items. At the bottom of the chain of command in the production team was the assistant stage manager Alison, who, after a Herculean effort scavenging around all the shops and nurseries in the area, managed to garner a fennel bulb in the posh greengrocer's shop in the lanes and some rosemary from her grandmother's garden. As far as the other items were concerned, she correctly deduced that no-one would know the difference and gathered together anything that was green and not easily identifiable. She tied the resultant greenery into bunches and tied them around the great bull's horns, just before it was hoisted into the air for the evening's performance. The fennel bulbs had been more difficult to incorporate, but believing that they were more easily identifiable than her herbal substitutes, she decided to make a feature of them and impaled them, artistically she thought with some pride, on the bull's horns.

It was in front of this random and bizarre collection of philosophers, vegetation and a bull that Zeus himself would have found impressive, that Hamlet had been briefed by Horatio about the ghost's previous visitations. The latter had just uttered the words "Look, my Lord – it comes!" As directed, both Horatio and Hamlet, perched on their two separate platforms downstage, were looking straight ahead over the heads of the audience towards a ghost which they heard and, as it were, created in its full majesty and horror behind the audience by their reactions to it. Amazement, fear and awe were what were required and they did their best to deliver those emotions as appropriate when the ghost spoke.

It was at precisely that moment, as they delivered the first of those appropriate expressions, that Daisy appeared through the swing doors behind the back of the set, causing Freud and Sophocles to swing wildly to and fro, as she forced her way through an opening in the back cloth.

For a brief moment, time seemed to stand still. The audience had, almost to a man, resigned themselves to enduring an evening of uninspiringly delivered "culture" for the sake of the promise of a banquet and free bar afterwards, and now they fell in to a frozen silence. Given the already bizarre staging of the piece and the style of its presentation, each person struggled in their own way to accommodate the arrival of a pantomime cow into the already challenging display in front of them. The more pretentious amongst them whispered to their partners of the wonderful juxtaposition of the sublime poetry of the Shakespearean language and the crude 'almost mediaeval' representation of the quasi–comedic bestiality of all human relationships. Others wrestled with the notion of the soft passivity of the cow as a paradigm for the role of women in a male dominated royal society – a notion that gathered strength when the dominant representation hanging above the cow was factored into the equation. However, for most of them, the struggle to provide an acceptable scenario for the advent on the battlements of Elsinore of a pantomime cow simply proved too much. Several members of the audience started to erupt in giggles and guffaws and were shushed irritably by those whose jaundiced opinions of modern theatre had led them to expect the excesses of designer theatre in the seemingly endless quest to explore hitherto un-trodden paths of invention. However, even their resolve wavered when, as Hamlet asked the spirit "Be thou a spirit of health or a goblin damn'd?" high in the air behind him, the cow winked suggestively, swished its tail and swayed its unnaturally pink and huge udders to and fro.

The actor playing Hamlet was a 'semi–professional', imported from a neighbouring town for the occasion. However, despite the programme notes which were somewhat economical with the truth, his professional experience was limited to an appearance on Hi–de–Hi as a yellow coat behind Su Pollard, who got covered in crazy foam, and an alien robot in Blake's 7. The remainder of his credits were exclusively amateur or the products of his fevered imaginings. He therefore did not have the breadth of experience that might alert him to take on board the possibility that the ripples of laughter might be caused by something untoward that was happening behind him.

He assumed first of all that his cod-piece had slipped, the Shakespearean equivalent of the classic fear experienced by all actors of appearing on stage with their flies undone. He checked. The codpiece was intact and properly located. But unfortunately in order to ascertain that fact, he clutched his private parts with frantic ferocity and scrutinised them balefully whilst asking

"Be thy intents wicked or charitable? Thou com'st in such a questionable shape – That I will speak to thee, I will call thee Hamlet!"

This stunningly un-princely behaviour stunned one half of the audience and delighted the growing numbers who were beginning to think that the evening was looking distinctly much more promising.

He lurched nervously through the rest of his first speech, as the cow, whose occupants were becoming more familiar with the controls were enjoying the distant laughter which they could hear greeting each fresh shimmy and wink. Unfortunately, the head was jammed so tightly over Gavin's own head that he was unable to hear more than a muffled approximation of speech from what he fondly imagined were a surprisingly distant Dame Trot and Simple Simon.

As Hamlet said "It waves me forth again, I'll follow it" the cows tail swished urgently and again the cow lowered one absurdly lashed lid and bent a rear leg coquettishly. Chance, that enemy of us all on occasion, so constructed events that every word spoken by the moody and introspective Dane was neatly counter-pointed by the dancing, prancing pair in the cow whose creative genius was warmly appreciated by their unseen and only dimly heard audience.

Horatio's experience of acting had been limited to a couple of comedies in his village hall involving vicars and trousers. He began to appreciate the unbridled mirth which greeted every utterance and was therefore overjoyed when his "What if it tempt you toward the flood my lord?" was greeted by whoops of joy, as unbeknownst to him, behind him the cow's udder squirted "milk" in all directions.

Hamlet, however, yearned not for laughter but fondly saw himself as a potentially great tragedian. His inexperience led him to start to bellow his lines in an attempt to drown out the creeping hysteria. When Horatio exited leaving Hamlet and "Daisy the Ghost" alone together, he was alerted to the reality of the situation by Sheila, the stage manager and thrust back onto the stage with the instruction to remove Daisy by force. Those were not the words she used, however.

It was then that farce turned to full–blooded slapstick.

Whilst the pre–recorded stentorian echoing tones of the ghost were relating the awful details of his untimely aural poisoning to the grieving and perplexed prince, the cow, whose occupants were now flagging somewhat, lurched in and out of grotesque and frenzied activity. Horatio climbed up to the rear dais at the back of the stage and seizing the halter of the cow, he attempted to drag it off. Gavin and Terry, mindful of the earlier threat of summary execution if they left the stage too soon, held firm and dug in their dainty cloven hooves. One horn came off in the hand of Horatio in the struggle and in his irritation he hurled it from him. Unfortunately, it hit Hamlet on the back of the head just as he was listening to the Ghost intoning the words '... Ay, that incestuous, that adulterate beast.' The Ghost was referring to his brother Claudius but Hamlet turned and saw an altogether different and more prosaic beast winking at him and being ridden like a wild-west bronco by his 'friend'

Horatio. Having identified what he saw as the source of all his misery, he bellowed with rage, slid down off his dais, ran to the back of the stage and began to climb the open work back cloth in order to reach the raised platform and eject the cow which had blighted his life. Worse, it had ruined his first ever chance to show Deirdre Ollerenshaw that he was worthy of more than her disdain. Throwing off any attempt to remain in character – indeed, how could he do otherwise? – blind rage got him half way up the fractured cut-out cloth before the weight proved too much for the supporting ropes.

The philosophers tumbled and the prancing polystyrene Godminster Bull itself fell in glorious slow motion landing impossibly and firmly on the back of the now spread-eagled Daisy who winked knowingly at the audience as she seemingly succumbed to the bull's amorous advances.

Hamlet then attacked Horatio, whose attempts to save the situation had been interpreted wrongly as encouraging the cow's worst excesses and their struggles projected Descartes off his plinth and caused it to swing across the stage and remove Daisy's head revealing the dazed Gavin within, who stood there stunned and blinking at the sudden explosion of light and noise.

At that moment a muffled but very audible voice from within the cow was heard to protest "You bastard, you promised you wouldn't do that!"

During these momentous events the tape had been relentlessly rolling on and the ghost boomed out its last lines – an injunction that none present would have any trouble obeying – "Adieu, adieu, Hamlet! Remember me!"

Rosita

Ramon Antonio Siffuentes awoke with a start.

For a few seconds he was disorientated, as his mind grappled with the flood of emotion and disjointed thoughts that tumbled through the fog of his slowly clearing brain.

He moved his head to the side of the thin pillow to avoid the brightness of the morning sun that cast an angled shadow across his bed. The momentary confusion of the beginning of each new little life that is another day rescued from the oblivion of sleep cleared and his heart lifted as he remembered.

Of course! It was today that Rosita della Chiesa was to be his at last. The months of waiting and uncertainty were over. Today, it was even more important than usual that everything should be done properly; that he should look and be at his best – for the incomparable Rosita. Nothing could be left to chance. He lay back upon the coarse cotton sheets and stared up at the rough plastered white ceiling that framed the elongated shadows cast there by the low early morning sun. The silhouette of the water jug on the chest in front of the casement windows suggested to his still-clearing mind the image of a woman kneeling at prayer. The curved handle of the pitcher being the arms raised to a bowed head.

He allowed himself the brief luxury of imagining Rosita at that moment. She too must be awakening on the other side of the town and she too must be thinking of what was to come in the hours ahead. Her face, that most beautiful face ever given to woman by a beneficent creator, would, despite the momentous significance of the day, surely retain that air of ethereal and detached calm which Ramon had always so admired. It was undoubtedly true, however, that the same look that enchanted him so, could, on occasion, provoke frustration and envy in the unworthy peons that encountered her in the streets and market place of their town. Even in the church, which she attended sometimes daily, there were those who struggled to accommodate the serene purity and devotion of this sublime woman within the context of their own venal lives.

But they could not possibly begin to understand or emulate her single minded devotion to God, virtue and duty, united as it was with a warm and open acceptance of all the joys that life has to bring.

Ramon pictured her head lying on the pillow. He realised with a small tremor of surprise that he had never seen her long, silky black hair flowing free. She always wore it pulled back from her face in loose braids or hidden under a head scarf of black lace. Both these styles, if possible, accentuated the pale serenity of the broad, oval face that framed her enormous and engagingly gentle brown eyes. It seemed to him that to be looked upon by Rosita was to be spiritually caressed by the gentle love that a beneficent God feels for his creation.

But at the same time, he knew beyond doubt that she herself was largely unaware of the startling and variable effect that she had on those who encountered her. She did not know, for instance, that even the otherwise most tolerant of women were disinclined to believe that her innocence could be as it seemed, nor was she aware that all men wanted those brown, brown eyes, that promised so much, to rest favourably upon them. It was a sad truth, he thought to himself, that such gentle beauty and innocence combined to provoke in the male ego a profound yearning to be the one man in all creation who can release the imagined passion within.

All her life she had been the unwilling and unknowing catalyst of trouble. It trailed in her wake like seagulls behind a fishing fleet. Men would look at her in open admiration and their women would feel diminished by their men's unspoken unfavourable comparison with them and react accordingly. Rosita's genuine lack of awareness of the power she exerted over others tended to exacerbate rather than diminish its effect.

But all that was going to change. Ramon was going to see to that. He understood Rosita. He recognised instinctively, and respected absolutely, her disarming simplicity and knew that it was in his power to protect her from the envy and the spite of the unworthy. He was a naturally modest and self–effacing man; but he knew with an absolute certainty that he and he alone could protect her from the unwanted effects of her natural but unlooked–for power to attract and confuse those around her.

In his semi–reverie, he pictured her rising from her bed. He saw the women with their blank, sun–worn faces outside her room, whispering together, and waiting for her to signal that she was ready for them to help her prepare for this most momentous of days. He tried not to imagine her in her bath as the women poured water over her. Tried not to think of the rivulets of fresh cool water, drawn that morning from the river, running down between her shoulder blades, over the pale olive skin, which he knew could only be soft and unblemished. Tried not to think of the droplets of water dripping from the long upward sweeping dark eyelashes onto the curve of her upper lip, which carried above it a faint down of fine hairs bleached by the sun. Tried not to think of those eyes, those dark pools of gentleness looking at him, through him to his very soul and welcoming what they saw there.

This wouldn't do. It was unseemly.

Ramon was a rare man. In many ways he was the exact opposite of Rosita.

Certainly, externally, his physical form was the antithesis of her graceful perfection. God had decreed that Ramon should be large and ungainly in appearance. His hair was black, like hers, but if he washed it and rubbed oil into it daily, it would never achieve the lustre that was hers naturally.

His body was broad at the shoulders and waist but not in proportion to his head, which was massive, square and had a pugnacious air, an air that was accentuated by the bushy sprouts of hair which freely decorated his eyebrows, ears and nostrils. The two latter growths he trimmed meticulously every day, aware of the effect of such simian characteristics upon the sensibilities of those whom he had always admired – people of taste and refinement.

His eyes, though not small, were made to appear so by the fact that the irises were unusually large and the remainder of the eye, which should have been white, was dominated by a suffusion of veins and blood vessels, which created the entirely false impression of a man inured to the excesses of alcohol. His skin was rough and slightly pitted by the evidence of an infantile bout of chicken pox. His face had a dark growth of bristles, which reappeared within an hour of his having shaved with the curved, bone handled cut throat razor that he wielded with surprising speed and accuracy. He was in all aspects but one, a bull of a man.

His hands however were surprisingly long and slender, with delicate, pale oval nails. Unlike the rest of his body they were unmarked by any blemish or evidence that might indicate that he earned his living by hard manual labour. They were, indeed, hands which might more properly have belonged to an artist and were used to good effect on his weekly visits to the Convent of Santa Maria, where he entertained the many orphans of the Revolution, who were in the good sisters' charge, by performing feats of sleight of hand which would have been the envy of many professional conjurers.

The good sisters knew him only as "O Urso Benevolo" – "The Benevolent Bear" – the silent and kindly man, who was seen at devotions regularly and spared time for the abandoned small ones in their charge. The nuns instinctively respected his desire for anonymity, although he had never given them cause to believe that he wouldn't answer any of their questions. It was as if they suspected that were they to question him too closely then he might be obliged to equivocate, if not dissemble, and they didn't want to put him in the embarrassing position of having to do so. His goodness was sufficiently evident to negate the demands of simple curiosity. Even the children accepted that their gentle benefactor entertained them in dumb show and it never, perhaps, occurred to them to challenge his evident desire to communicate only with his marvellously eloquent, dancing hands and the smile of affection that illuminated his broad face when in their company.

Those self-same hands that could produce coins seemingly from thin air were now scooping cold rainwater from the bowl by the open window and splashing it over his face. He surveyed his flawed countenance in the fly–blown chipped gilt mirror hanging on the bedroom wall. A momentary betrayal of the tiniest doubt of his worthiness to be the man who would deprive all other men of the chance to possess Rosita flickered across his face – to be replaced by a resolve to suppress those feelings and honour and embrace the destiny that God and fate had placed before him. Unhurriedly, and with a precision that an observer might consider to be at odds with his considerable bulk, he continued his preparation for the day that would bind them together, before God and man, forever. He took the new crisp white shirt from its cellophane wrapping and placed the pins carefully in a bowl on the wooden table. From a box in the drawer under that table he took out the plain gold cufflinks that his father had worn when he had married his mother all those years ago. Ramon had only worn them a very few times in his life. They were for special occasions and he had experienced few of those in his life. He then carefully pressed the dark linen suit which he had last worn at the funeral of Rico Pessoa, some months ago. The ladies of the town laundry would have been impressed by the result. Not a crease or wrinkle marred the surface of the only garments he possessed that might be described as suitable for a formal occasion. As his deft passes with the iron tamed the linen jacket, his mind was drawn back to the ferocious storm that had marred both the sombre interment of Pessoa and Ramon's suit on that last occasion that he had worn it.

The late (and largely unlamented) Rico had been the owner of the abattoir and meat packing plant that provided what employment there was to be had in the sprawling and decaying town. Rico had never, in a life devoted to the ruthless pursuit of self-advancement, failed to take advantage of his position and of the weaknesses and fears of others. Men who had little in their lives already had slowly withered inside as a direct result of the certain knowledge (in some cases) and leaden suspicion (in others) that their wives and daughters would inevitably, at some time, have been the target of Rico's casual and violent lust. The women never spoke of it to their men. Despite having been so vilely abused, they had that devotion shown by women in the face of all manner of personal violation that led them to protect their husbands and children from the inevitable result of sharing that burden with their families. They knew they had to protect their men and their livelihood. This conspiracy of silence avoided the risk of losing their homes, their jobs and their small remaining dignity.

The men sublimated their suspected but unspoken emasculation in the consumption of cheap alcohol. There was no other way to salvage their honour without the inevitable danger of depriving their children of food or even, at worst ... a father.

But Pessoa's sudden death had changed little in the town. There is always another Rico Pessoa to step into the breach, just as when a cure is found for a disease another even more virulent strain will soon replace it. The few who control the power and the money rarely allow a hiccup like a petty dictator's demise to shake their hands far from the reins of influence, or the pockets of the poor, or the bodies of their womenfolk.

Ramon sighed heavily and brought his thoughts back to the business of the day. He hung his now immaculately pressed suit over the high back of his grandfather's upright chair and set to, polishing his shoes. He had not eaten any breakfast, but had drunk only rainwater scooped from the barrel outside his window. He wondered if Rosita had an appetite this morning or whether the nervous anticipation of the day ahead would send a surge of adrenaline that would subdue the desire to eat. He decided that she would, despite a probable inclination to the contrary, eat sparingly, in order to prevent any faintness that might otherwise arise and which might falsely indicate to others that she was in any way nervous about the day ahead.

As he carefully buffed yet again his already mirror-shiny black shoes, he fancied that by now the women would be laying out Rosita's pure white dress and combing her equally pure black hair, teasing out the tangles and increasing the natural gloss with every pass of their combs. She would be silent and composed and the women would respect that silence, whilst exchanging brief and eloquent glances behind her back. The women were all aware, despite the familiarity acquired over the years of performing these rituals for others, that this time it was different. Rosita was different, but they wouldn't understand how or why. However hard they tried they would be incapable of understanding Rosita, and, despite being good women by most accepted standards, they would most certainly resent that.

Before dressing, Ramon shaved, the long bone-handled blade sweeping in elegant curves over his awkwardly contoured face. Despite the terrain it was compelled to cross the fiercely sharp blade drew not a speck of blood, such was the dextrous use of those elegant hands. When he had finished, he flicked the last of the soap off the razor, carefully washed and dried it and then commenced to hone its edge to an even wickeder sharpness He then carefully laid it on the embroidered white cotton cloth that lay at the precise centre of the scrubbed wooden table beside his bed.

Having dressed, he knelt before the simple crucifix that hung on the wall opposite the window. By now the shafts of light were slightly shorter and faintly illuminated the crown of thorns on the head of the dead saviour.

The tapering fingers of his right hand touched his forehead, breast and left and right shoulders in a blur of movement, as he whispered, in a voice that sounded as if it were coming from the depths of the earth: "Lord – make me worthy."

He remained on his knees for several long moments, staring at the broken image of Jesus on the cross. Then he took a long deep breath, crossed himself once again and rose resolutely to his feet. He went to the mirror and surveyed himself with no satisfaction, but to check that everything was "proper." He took out a clean handkerchief from the drawer and carefully, with thumb and forefinger inside the handkerchief wiped the corners of his downward turning mouth, removing the flecks that had the habit of accumulating there. He discarded the handkerchief and tucked two more fresh ones into his trouser pockets along with his rosary beads.

The time had come.

Rosita della Chiesa was to be his and she must not be kept waiting.

As he stepped out of his small house on the hillside and turned to lock the door, he recalled his first sight of Rosita. His natural instinct to seek out places where he could be totally anonymous had led him one Sunday to a church on the other side of town that he had never attended before – the monastery of San Miguel. Rosita was turning from the Communion rail hands clasped together in prayer, eyes downcast. She had walked past him and, as she passed, she had left in the air a beguiling hint of incense, mingled with strong soap and olive oil and something else that was hers and hers alone – an indefinable sweetness that seemed to complement the other more recognisable, mundane aromas and transcend them.

He felt at that moment something he had never felt before. Something that was as unexpected as it was compelling. A need, a connection, a ... something ....that was directly related to another human being. He was unable to identify at that moment the precise nature of that connection but he nonetheless recognised it as essential to his future well–being. Breaking with his habit of visiting different places of worship, he became a regular member of the congregation of the monastery of San Miguel. He attended mass at least two or three times a week and benediction on Fridays. It was rare that he did not glimpse Rosita there too.

The first time their eyes met was the first moment of pure joy that Ramon had ever experienced. They each held the gaze for longer than would be normally acceptable. He did so out of a kind of paralysis of euphoria – a sensation of floating outside of space or time.

Her reasons for doing so were less clear, until she smiled at him, openly and warmly, without a hint of the coquette or a suggestion of impropriety. It was as if there was a recognition by each of them of the rightness of their exchanging the simple acknowledgement, that the other was there and was looking back with warmth and openness. He remembered feeling that he finally knew what a state of grace was. He immediately reprimanded himself for the blasphemy of that thought, before re-assessing what had happened. It was no blasphemy! Her look and her smile were open, warm and sincere – as if she recognised him as a friend and felt safe and unthreatened by this stranger she had encountered in the house of God.

It had never occurred to Ramon that such a person might exist in any way that impinged on his life, and certainly not a woman as improbably beautiful as Rosita. He learnt her name when she was addressed by the priest as she left after benediction one summer evening. Even though he had not considered what her name might be, he was unsurprised when he heard it. He felt that nothing about her could surprise him ever. Even her name seemed appropriate and almost inevitable, once he had heard it. Rosita.

As the months passed the smiles became longer, the unspoken spiritual intimacy deepened and developed...
... and then...
... today, on the feast of Santa Lucia, they were to be united for ever before God.

Ramon's car was waiting for him. He walked slowly along the dry and cracked sandy track that led down from the side of the hill that was scattered with white and cream single storey homes, all of which looked as if they had been thrown there many years ago by the hand of a bored giant who had then moved on without a second thought for their random arrangement in the most inaccessible abutments and outcrops. Ramon crossed the wooden bridge with the broken hand-rail that spanned the thin, muddy trickle that was once a tributary of the river that flowed through the town. The construction of Pessoa's packing plant had necessitated the diversion of the once clean and swiftly flowing water, which he and his father had fished many years ago. It was now used to cool the machinery and sluice the floors of the abattoir, before disappearing underground with its grim evidence. No one cared, it seemed, that the terrain had been so savagely raped by Pessoa. He had offered jobs to the poor and advancement to the managerial and clerical classes. He had appointed the Chief of Police. What was the loss of a little fishing and irrigation of a few olive groves in the face of the march of progress?

Ramon slipped carefully into the back seat of the car and nodded to the driver in the mirror. No words were exchanged, as they drove towards the town along dry, dirty roads that were rutted and potholed. He watched a single buzzard circling above the higher reaches of the hills where scrawny goats searched for scraps of dry vegetation causing the bells around their necks to mark out their tinny, clanking progress.

The leather upholstery of the car was pitted with the evidence of the car's previous occupants – men who felt the need to assert the superiority of their positions by a studied carelessness with cigarette and cigar butts. Men whose shoes had not been as clean as his when they sprawled full length on the bench seat.

He had resisted the almost overwhelming urge to go and see Rosita the previous evening. His notion of what was and was not proper had overruled this untypical bout of impetuousness. Nothing, he decided, must detract from the purity of the moment of their union. He suppressed his need to reassure her that he would be there for her, her rock for the rest of her life. She would know that, he reasoned, as soon as she saw him there and their eyes met.

He was accustomed to sleeping well, so had been surprised that his anticipation of this day had fractured his night with bouts of wakefulness that he had never experienced before.

As they entered the narrow streets of the town, Ramon asked the driver to stop and wait for him outside the gates of the market. He went into the lanes that were full of women who had risen early to get fresh fish and meat, none of which was abundantly available and would be sold out before the sun had risen much further in the cloudless sky. As he approached the flower stall at the top of the cobbled lane, he saw the stooped form of the flower-seller automatically bending to pull a bunch of tall lilies out of the brass jug that held them. He put out a restraining hand.

Ramon was a regular customer. He always bought the same flowers and took them to the cemetery on the south of the town to place upon his parents' grave. He had done so for twenty or more years and, kneeling by the plain wooden cross, would share with them more than he had ever confided in any living soul – his hopes and his fears, his loneliness and then his eventual and welcome discovery that they were not the only people that he could love. There was another. He had been an only child and his parents had both, in their different ways, shown him the joy that could be derived from a relationship that was based on love – both for each other and for their creator. His father took the awkward young boy with him when he went fishing or to pick olives. He taught him all that he knew about the natural world around them and the dangers of the world that was evolving in their town. His mother could make a nourishing and even tasty meal from ingredients that seemed frugal and unappetising. She told the young Ramon stories of princesses and ogres, of knights on horseback who rode to the succour of the oppressed and downtrodden. And both his parents were devoted to the service of God and their community. Today he was not visiting their graves, however, he had told them already, when he last brought them the lilies that his mother had so loved, of Rosita, of his happiness and their future.

Today, he selected a single yellow rose. And did not flinch when the large denomination note he proffered elicited a demand from the aged and bent flower seller for two more such notes. He returned with the precious flower secure in a twist of brown paper to the waiting car. The driver continued to stare impassively ahead in silence, as Ramon settled into the back seat again to complete the journey.

Every detail of the predominantly grimy and poverty stained streets through which they passed seemed to him clearer than they had ever been before. It was as if the streets, or Ramon's perception of them, had been somehow clarified by the quiet sense of elation that he felt in his gradual progress towards Rosita.

The now dusty black limousine drew into the square in front of the Monastery of San Miguel. Ramon ducked out and thanking the driver, without a backward glance walked slowly up the steps and through the small opening in the foot of one of the vast and closed doors, which years of grime carried by the winter mists had blackened and pitted. His shoes tapped out hollow sounding double echoes on the chipped mosaic floor, as he walked towards the altar to kneel before the faded, gilded rail until the appointed hour. He was very early as was his habit in life.

Rosita's eyes were tightly closed as she knelt beside her bed in prayer. As Ramon had rightly suspected, she had initially declined the offers of fruit, dried meats and bread. Apprehension had diminished her appetite and it seemed wasteful to her to eat in those circumstances. However, she had relented in the face of their continued insistence, which was distracting her from her prayers and efforts at self-composure.

Her apprehension was caused not by any doubt as to her ultimate and complete happiness – that was without question and assured – but solely by her concern that she should fall victim to a sudden doubt or sense of loss for the part of her life which she was about to surrender, willingly but irrevocably and eternally, in order to achieve that happiness.

There was a knock on the door and the Abbot, Monsignor Pio, was shown into the bare room where she was kneeling. He was an austere man, rarely moved to any emotional response to the secular and muddled lives of his flock, preferring to worship his God through solitary contemplation and wrestling with the challenge of reconciling the intellectual and spiritual worlds. The worlds physical and emotional he allowed to intrude into his life as little as possible. He had been sent by the head of his order to take charge of the Monastery, its monks and its congregation. He saw the latter responsibility as a cross he had to bear to achieve salvation. His preference would have been to contemplate the greatness of God through quiet study of the scriptures rather than through the very real involvement with the lives of his parishioners.

He was therefore a reluctant participant in the proceedings of the day, which promised to combine the worlds spiritual and temporal in a particularly ceremonial way. His reluctance was increased by the fact that he had, most untypically, noticed and been intrigued by, both of the two people who were to take centre stage.

Despite his rigid mantle of asceticism, he was not completely immune to the disturbing effects of Rosita's powerful combination of piety and external beauty. Indeed, it was the inescapable air of true goodness that pervaded every fibre of her being that, perversely, he found the most disturbing. It was a goodness that had nothing to do with religious theory or the awareness of God through the study of scripture. It was real and tangible and complete and made him feel – in a way that he did not care to examine too closely – inadequate. He was also aware, in a more detached and objective way, that, were he to be susceptible to of any form of physical attraction, it might very well be directed towards this woman that knelt in prayer before him – this creature that so splendidly reflected the true spirit of her creator. He would not have been able to recognise many of the congregation that regularly attended services at his monastery. But he recognised Rosita. And he also recognised Ramon, who unsettled the Abbot even more, albeit for very different reasons.

The Abbot knelt beside Rosita and bowed his head. After they had prayed together he rose and straightened his coarsely woven brown woollen cassock, which was lined with soft cotton to accommodate the Abbot's unfortunate allergy to wool. He surprised himself by offering her his hand so that she might also rise to her feet. She murmured her thanks, as he tried to identify the aroma that wafted past him as she stood.

The odour of sanctity, perhaps? – he mused, before a flash of self–irritation prompted him to re–arrange his features back to the detached and generalised benevolence that he considered appropriate for such occasions. Fortunately nobody in the room, it seemed, had been aware of the momentary distraction which had allowed his guard to be so unintentionally lowered.

He waited by the door as Rosita warmly clasped the hand of the oldest of the attendant ladies.

"Thank you for your kindness – may God bless you!"

Martita Magiore, lowered her head slowly as if in quiet acceptance of the blessing.

The Abbot led Rosita from the room to her destiny.

As she entered the vast echoing space, the Abbot stood aside to allow her to walk unattended towards the broad back of the man who stood alone at its centre. When she was a few feet away, he turned slowly and their eyes met.

Those who were present that day would never and could never understand what then happened. A look of unalloyed joy spread like sunlight across Rosita's face. She opened her mouth as if to speak, to voice her surprise and relief – but, instead, she closed her mouth again, nodded in approval and composed herself.

The Executioner and the Condemned never took their eyes off each other as Ramon went about his business with careful and loving precision. It seemed a moment so private that no–one intervened, when her arms remained unbound, when no hood was offered; its refusal would have been in no doubt. The noose was placed around her smooth and flawless neck as gently and ceremonially as a garland of flowers, but still Ramon did not lay his hands directly upon her.

For an eternal second, their eyes locked with an intensity of communication that many lovers never achieve in a long lifetime of togetherness. Her hands held a yellow rose to her bosom, which she lifted to her lips as she nodded her assent, almost conspiratorially.

Ramon, State Executioner of the People's Revolutionary Republic, carried out the sentence of the Courts that Rosita della Chiesa be hanged by the neck until dead for the murder of Rico Pessoa.

Rosita had chosen this fate as the only alternative to the one that Rico had had in mind for her. She had never, for a second, doubted that the very people who would benefit most from the evil Pessoa's descent into eternal damnation would be the ones who could not under any circumstances allow her to survive. There could be no admission of responsibility or guilt by the ruling class, although they were all as guilty as Pessoa for the atrocities he had been allowed to commit to the town, its businesses and its people. That way would lie counter–revolution and anarchy. Rosita had accepted that as the inevitable price of her sanity and her spiritual freedom.

Ramon stared blankly, straight ahead, as if in a trance, at the space where Rosita's face had been while the official doctor went down to the dark room below to certify that she was indeed dead. He did not look down at her mortal remains, as he slowly left the room. His mind's eye was focused intently and calmly on the bone handled razor that lay on the white embroidered cloth on the table beside his bed. As the faint aroma that he had learnt to associate with his Rosita slowly faded to nothingness, he realised for the first time that they had never, at any time, spoken a single word to each other, yet there had been a total and mutual understanding that transcended anything that words could ever possibly convey.

He was impatient to join her. He had no doubt of a merciful God's forgiveness of what he had done and what he intended to do.

Part II
Other Worlds

A Tourist Invasion

The Oox (whose name in their own language translated as "the supreme enlightened ones who communicate using an harmonious low pitched modulation") did not like the Iix. 'Iix' was a word in the Oox language meaning "despicable beings of very little merit who communicate in a most unpleasant high–pitched, squeaky and thoroughly obnoxious modulation." The language of the Oox was in fact considerably more sophisticated than were the Oox themselves.

Not unsurprisingly the Iix referred to themselves in their own similarly subtle language as the "Khee" – "delightfully light–toned beings of impeccable taste and appearance," whereas the self–styled "Oox" were, to the Iix, the "Khoogh" – "gratingly heavy toned eaters of daarg–droppings."

The Khee were more than a little hypocritical in this reference to their enemies, as they themselves would have been more than happy to consume daarg–droppings every minute of their sixteen second day, if they had had the opportunity to do so. Unfortunately, for them, daargs were only to be found in the land of the Oox. Daarg droppings were a much coveted delicacy. In fact, the only species that could resist daarg–droppings were the daargs themselves, who couldn't understand what all the fuss was about, but much appreciated the double advantage of being offered copious supplies of food by all and sundry and not having to worry about the tedious business of waste–disposal. In fact, in the entire universe there was, it is believed, no other species whose arrival in a flower bed to scratch about and squat with a look of intense concentration on their faces did not provoke bellowed imprecations and missiles from the owners of said flower beds.

Occasionally an unusually enlightened Khee or Oox, to use the names by which each race referred to itself, would attain brief prominence in their respective societies and argue that, aside from what was, after all, the minor matter of a slight variation in the pitch of their voices, there were no other discernible differences between their races. Indeed, a gathering of mute Oox and Khee would have no means of distinguishing one from another, apart perhaps from the faint odour of daarg droppings emanating from the Oox. But the idea of any rapprochement always fell on deaf, or rather too highly tuned, ears.

Over many generations of border disputes, skirmishes and minor wars, both races had survived in a state of fluctuating parity. But that was all about to change. The Khee had invented the Megahurts – a biotechnical crypto–organic "loudspeaker" of gargantuan size that was designed to resonate at a frequency unbearable and even fatal to Oox sense and sensibility. The Khee had been engaged for some time in the process of trundling this massive structure slowly towards a point on the Oox borders, where it would be capable of being aimed and focussed to inflict maximum damage upon their hated enemies. Meanwhile, the Oox were deploying a highly toxic nerve gas that they had been working on for hours and hours (bear in mind the length of their days). This fatal toxin would be activated only by the very precise spectrum of frequencies emanating from Khee vocal chords. It would then cause their throats to contract rapidly and deprive them of access to the air that both species breathed.

It seemed that the internecine war which had occupied their every millisecond for generations was about to reach a climax that would result in the annihilation of one or other or both races, depending on which of them deployed their particularly nasty weapons of mass destruction the soonest.

There was not even the opportunity given in most wars throughout the universe for one side to capitulate in the face of impossible odds and take the consequences of surrender. Such was the reciprocal hatred inbred into the Khee and the Oox that complete victory over their enemy meant only the total destruction and removal from their planet of that enemy. There was no room for negotiation or small concessions.

If their respective leaders had even considered advancing for a parley, they would have been so enraged at the mere sound of each other's voices they would have set upon each other with unimaginable ferocity. They couldn't even benefit from the scenario beloved of story tellers throughout the civilised universe – the one where the prince of one warring tribe falls head over heels in love with the princess of the despised enemy. The Khee and Oox were hermaphroditic self-replicating beings for whom attraction and romantic love were concepts as alien as carrot juice was to the sixth incarnation of the Time Lord known as the Doctor.

Speaking of which remarkable and noble being...

The Doctor and Peri had been on Tribolyca for only a brief time but it had seemed much longer. The Tribolycanna were obsessively hospitable and terminally garrulous. It was universally acknowledged that before enquiring as to a Tribolycan's health, you should ensure that you had a packed lunch and the ability to retain an interested expression on your face for a considerable time. Follow-up questions were a decidedly bad idea. In fact, questions were best avoided altogether. However the Doctor had felt constrained to come to their aid when he had discovered that their genetic inability to refuse hospitality was being abused by an Earth based travel agency offering very competitive, cheap holidays for the deaf and hard of hearing (on the very sensible basis that any other group of tourists would subsequently sue for damages for boredom).

Selachos Bdella Travel Inc. were able to do this and realise a massive profit, as their only cost was the travel to Tribolyca; all accommodation and food being provided free by the Tribolycanna. But as theirs was not a planet rich in either mineral resources or the ingredients of food, the Doctor felt that a limited intervention to protect them from exploitation and ultimate extinction was not unjustifiable.

At first, the Doctor attempted to persuade the Tribolycanna to solve their own problem by the simple expedient of refusing hospitality to the tourists. Their reply (abbreviated for the reader's benefit from its original three hour length) was to the effect that even though they were aware that they were being comprehensively mugged, they were no more capable of denying hospitality to a traveller than were the inhabitants of Chaite of having a haircut. Never having heard of Chaite or its hirsute (or bald?) inhabitants, the Doctor, whose innate curiosity often led him to investigate further where wiser travellers might shuffle off to Buffalo, longed to enquire further but forbore out of consideration for his travelling companion, Peri, who was becoming visibly and audibly impatient. (Humans' shorter life span made them incapable of enjoying a really good conversation, he often thought).

The Doctor had eventually solved the problem, rather neatly in his own rather biased opinion, by immersing a slow–release sulphur "bomb" in the network of warm springs on Tribolyca's Costa del Algol, which caused the immediate and hasty departure of the tourists and the subsequent bankrupting of Selachos Bdella Inc. The Tribolycanna, mercifully, had no sense of smell and were only aware that their geysers were now of a different and (to them) most pleasant hue. In fact, at their earnest request, the Doctor had contrived to add other chemicals and dyes to a selection of the planet's geysers so that the sixteen colours of the Tribolycannan spectrum were represented at different locations throughout the planet. Future generations would thrill to the great work and it became legendary to the extent that annual festivals were held for thousands of years to celebrate the 'colouring of the waters' that led to the great age of enlightenment on Tribolyca. The festival lasted for days and concluded with a performance of 'The Eulogy to the Doctor' – a shortened version of which was read aloud to children at bed time and was very effective at lulling the little darlings into a most deep sleep within minutes.

As the TARDIS door swung shut behind them, abruptly cutting off the continuing and insistent chorus of gratitude from the beguiling but exhausting Tribolycanna, Peri took a deep breath of comparatively fresh air and stared accusingly at the Doctor. "I don't suppose it occurred to you to warn me that you were intending to create the biggest stink-bomb in the Universe! I didn't know whether to stick my fingers in my ears for relief from their incessant wittering or to hold my nose! What's next? A guided tour of a volcano? Tea with Torquemada?"

"No, he makes a terrible cup of tea. Never warms the pot," grinned the Doctor. "No, Peri, I've been thinking for a long time that we deserve a little treat. I am going to take you somewhere that will dispel all memories of sulphur fountains and loquacious Tribolycanna. And I know just the place that will lighten your mood and put a bit of joy in your life..." he added as he launched himself at the TARDIS console.

And so it was that they found themselves standing on a small green island in the middle of a vast expanse of blue sea gazing at a sky filled with a myriad of interconnecting and pulsating rainbows which revolved around a vortex of such incandescent beauty that Peril could only gasp with wonder

After standing in blissful silence for a long time, Peri turned to the Doctor with her eyes wide open in stunned disbelief and joy. She looked at him and slowly asked

"Not the Eye of Orion?... At last!"

He nodded down at her indulgently, with only the slightest trace of a triumphant smirk.

After the TARDIS had left its vantage point some hours later, the travellers were unaware that where it had stood were the crushed and obliterated remains of the entire civilisations of the Oox and the Khee, their armies, their cities and their people.

In case the fate of the daargs concerns you – they are and remain burrowing creatures who were all curled up safely underground when the bellicose admirers of their by-product met their swift quietus. They were only slightly irritated when they had to make other arrangements for the disposal of their droppings and, with only that minor inconvenience to overcome have learned to enjoy their solitary occupation of their world, free from the constant noise and destruction caused by the Oox and the Khee.

Parasites Regained

"I won't be a minute!" the Doctor had exclaimed before bounding out of the TARDIS console room with that deceptive speed that he could muster when he wanted to in times of urgency or stress, but that seemed alien to him the rest of the time. That sudden departure had been what seemed hours ago to Peri, so she went off to search the limitless inner reaches of the little blue box that had recently become her home.

She had been looking for him for quite some time when she came upon a large handwritten sign bearing the legend, "Go Away! – Extreme Danger," hanging on the handle of a door that she hadn't come across before in the labyrinth of passages that radiated from the TARDIS control room. It was half way down a corridor which, it had to be admitted, looked remarkably similar to every other corridor in the TARDIS. It was also next door to the 'Gymnasium', a facility that she had had no reason to expect to find in the TARDIS, given her experience thus far of the fitness and apparent health of the Doctor. On opening the door of the 'Gymnasium' she had discovered that the interior was, as she might have guessed, devoid of anything that could be remotely considered as capable of stimulating the heart–rate – unless you lived in morbid fear of a half–strung tennis racket, a pair of grass stained cricket trousers and a strange twisted wooden object with a long–deflated and decaying balloon at one end and a rather nasty spike at the other, upon whose purpose and function Peri chose not to speculate.

Leaving the musty and unused gym, Peri returned to survey the message hanging from the adjacent door.

After reflection she decided to take the plunge and defy the message on the sign, partly because it lacked the formality of a printed warning and bore all the evidence of having been scrawled in haste by someone who was perhaps trying to hide something – or even themselves. She opened the door and saw another door in front of her, with a similar notice attached to it that read: "You have been warned. GO AWAY!" Having learned over the years that faint heart never won fair anything, she cautiously peered around it and saw the Doctor flicking intently through a mammoth leather bound volume that he had presumably plucked from one of the many shelves that lined the long walls of what was very obviously the TARDIS Library – something else that she had not discovered before, but which was a less surprising find than the gymnasium. The hand that wasn't flicking the yellowing pages of the book was holding something that looked suspiciously like a cream doughnut for the brief second she glimpsed it before he stuffed it under a pile loose paper on the table.

"Can't you read?" he threw over his shoulder, in that aggressive manner adopted by people who feel guilty about something and want to get in first before they're accused themselves. In order to forestall any further discussion on that subject or his dietary lapse – and before she could confirm that she did indeed possess that very useful skill, which was why she just might have appreciated knowing about the existence of the Library, he continued, "Anyway, no time to waste, follow me!" He plucked his awful jacket off the back of the chair, tucked the volume under his arm and strode off towards the TARDIS' console room muttering darkly to himself.

Peri set off after him asking, "What's so urgent, and what's that huge book? And where are we going now?"

"Everything, my address book and Vertipax," he replied, as he arrived at the console and threw many switches in quick succession. Peri was convinced that at least half of them did nothing more useful other than serve to impress and bamboozle those who were susceptible to such technological flamboyance.

When, after a series of lurches, bumps and a moment of vertigo, they emerged from the TARDIS, Peri saw that they had materialised outside what the manufacturers of tin shacks would be deeply offended to have credited as one of their products.

'Dilapidated' was as accurate a description of this structure as 'large–ish' would be of the Palace of Versailles. Before Peri could express her forebodings, which were principally stimulated by her very keen sense of smell, the Doctor had thrown open (and then away – when it came off in his hand) the flimsy door and entered.

Inside, a predominantly green, partially humaniform and disturbingly moist creature was introduced to Peri as "... my old friend, Mosca Ragazzo." The Doctor sat down on something that looked as if it had been constructed of wood a thousand years earlier by a visually impaired axe–wielding maniac and never cleaned since. He then produced a pile of photographs, which Peri glimpsed only briefly as the creature scrutinised them, (that is if waving half a dozen antennae in the general direction of something could be defined as scrutinising it) and then Mosca led the Doctor off into the interior of the hovel twittering and twirling his antennae as he went. Peri was about to follow but thought better of it. It seemed that the aroma intensified as she stepped further into Mosca's shack and she was barely able to restrain herself from gagging standing by the door. Despite her curiosity she decided to remain where she was. There was a distant crash, the sound of heavy objects being dragged around, a surprised squeal or two from some creature whose identity Peri could only guess at, and the Doctor reappeared with Mosca following dragging a large bright red box.

Mosca crooned at the box and a lid slid open. Reaching in Mosca retrieved a small shiny object and handed it (or 'pseudopoded' it) to the Doctor, who proceeded to wrap it in what looked suspiciously like one of his old shirts and popped it into his pocket. She had noticed in the short time that she had been with this very strange man that his pockets seemed to have the same properties as the TARDIS itself, in that he seemed to be able to produce a seemingly endless series of disparate objects from it when the occasion demanded. A swift whispered conversation ensued between Mosca and the Doctor in a language that Peri had never heard before, if indeed it was a language, and she had a moment of suspicion and surprise, as the TARDIS' normally useful function of rendering all languages comprehensible to its occupants seemed to have failed. Was this deliberate she wondered? Was the Doctor trying to hide something from her? At last, and to her immense relief, they left the foul smelling and decidedly unhealthy quarters of the Doctor's 'good friend' Mosca. They regained the fresh air and she had her first opportunity to properly take in her surroundings. The Doctor unwrapped the small shiny object and inserted it into a small mobile drone that looked to Peri exactly like a jukebox on legs, except that no tune was forthcoming. As soon as the drone jerked into life, she witnessed the bizarre sight a score of small, driverless tractors speeding into the TARDIS bearing packing cases on the way in and exiting empty. Peri's insistent queries were repeatedly ignored or impatiently dismissed by the Doctor.

"Not now, Peri, can't you see I'm busy!" What he was busy doing defeated her, as he seemed to be just standing there watching proceedings with a self-satisfied smile upon his face.

It was only after they had returned to the TARDIS and left Vertipax, that the Doctor suddenly and innocently turned to Peri and said benignly,

"Well, that was a good day's work, wouldn't you say? I was rather pleased with that."

"I'm sure I might agree with you there, Doctor, if I had the faintest clue about what has been going on! You haven't said a word to me all day. You marched me off to the nastiest, yuckiest hovel I have ever set foot in and beyond introducing me to its smelly occupant you haven't felt the need to include me in anything!" protested Peri to the Doctor's back, as he strode off towards the Library. He stopped and turned round with a look on his face that was difficult to decipher. Was it resignation? Impatience? Or realisation that she had a point? You never knew with the Doctor. Despite all his infuriating habits and unpredictable actions, he always had good reasons for what he did and possibly even for not sharing what those reasons were at the time. But none of that was always easy to live with and right now Peri wanted answers.

"Well, what would you like to know? All you have to do is ask you know. I may have many remarkable talents, if I am to believe what others say about me, but mind–reading certainly isn't one of them."

Peri knew better than to argue.

"Well", she said, "let's start with an explanation of everything that has happened since I found you in here with your 'address book'."

"I'll have to take you back little earlier than that if you really want to understand what happened just now," replied the Doctor.

"I'll have to take you back to long before the Time Lords looked outward from Gallifrey, to a time when a race called the Vervalloochenen established Vertipax to monitor what they saw as the destructive threat of pollution in the Universe. Planetary systems would be checked every three or four thousand years and any pollution that threatened the continued existence of a planet or planetary system would be eradicated..."

"Hurrumph! We could do with them on Earth," interrupted Peri.

"Mmmm, yes, well I'll be coming to that." said the Doctor. "You remember those short trips we made to Earth recently..."

"How could I forget landing twenty or thirty times in quick succession and waiting here while you sashayed outside with what looked like a vacuum cleaner and, as usual, declined to share with me what you were doing, let alone why you were doing it?"

"Sashayed?" interrupted the Doctor. "Did I really 'sashay'? I don't think I've ever done that before? How does 'sashaying' differ from walking, which is what I thought I was doing at the time? Or is it just one of your interminable Americanisms?"

"Don't play word games with me Doctor! You know perfectly well what I mean. Why are you still refusing to tell me? Don't you think I am entitled to an explanation? Are you tired of having me around? Is that it? If so, just say so and you can drop me off somewhere. Preferably not – what did you call it? Yes – Vertipax – preferably not Vertipax, but even that might be preferable to being treated like this!"

She paused for breath. As she did so the Doctor took a deep breath himself and nodded in acknowledgement of the justice of her complaint. But his face continued to betray his reluctance to satisfy her curiosity.

"I was only protecting you, Peri. Sometimes it's better for you that you don't know exactly what's going on. I would have hoped that by now you might trust me a little more but I can see that I don't always help you to do that. I'm sorry." And she had to admit that at that moment he did seem to be genuinely apologetic.

She smiled at him in mute encouragement for him to continue – and waited.

"And of course, what you don't know can't leap out of your shoes one day and bite your nose off, as the saying goes."

"What saying? I've never heard that one before..."

"Will you stop interrupting, Peri, and listen to me? You did ask for an explanation and I am giving you one. It will be easier if you just listen for once!"

He paused and she bit her lip to prevent herself from a riposte.

The Doctor, mollified by her silence, continued,

"Anyway... I was just planting a little circumstantial evidence to help my friend Mosca Ragazzo. I'm afraid that the noble intentions of the Vervalloochenen that I mentioned just now... well, I'm afraid that their good intentions became somewhat diluted and even distorted over the intervening millennia and their descendants and successors in their enterprise have subcontracted what they still consider to be a worthwhile, but somewhat onerous task. A long way down the lengthy subcontracting chain is Mosca, who calls himself an entrepreneur, though others might accord him a less flattering description. Being a creature with a sharp eye for a good deal, he was naturally delighted when I offered to go to Earth and tidy up a little pollution problem on his behalf – especially as he immediately sensed that he could make a sizeable profit on the deal."

Peri interrupted "But what on Earth were you doing with the vacuum cleaner, Doctor?"

"Aaaah, they weren't vacuum cleaners, Peri, though I do admit, now you come to mention it, that they bear a passing resemblance to those antique domestic devices of your period on Earth. They are, in fact, atmosphere redistribution generators" added the Doctor, "I was simply re–arranging selected local topography. A few crops here and there, flattened into neat little circles, ellipses and other geometric shapes that precisely mimic the effect of Mosca's craft landing on Earth to prove to those who contracted Mosca to do the job that his ships had been there and fulfilled the terms of his contract by eliminating the pollution. I chose that kind of terrain to provide easily recognisable identifying marks for the automated long range inspection process. Of course, the local inhabitants who discovered these marks would undoubtedly have made a song and dance about 'alien craft' having landed, but they would have been dismissed as fruit cases."

"Nut," corrected Peri, "or... cake."

"Don't you ever think of anything but food?" the Doctor snapped at her.

"Please don't interrupt! Anyway... the preternaturally venal Mosca was very pleased with the 'evidence' of his job well done which I offered him in those photographs and paid up eagerly. Unfortunately, he wouldn't have trusted me if I had offered to fill in for him for nothing, which I would happily have done, but he couldn't resist the opportunity of bettering me on a deal. So I offered him a deal which I knew he would find attractive, as he wouldn't know that I knew the true value to him of the crop circle ploy compared to the actual cost of his going to Earth and doing the job himself. So that is why you saw all those packages being loaded into the store room."

"What's in them, Doctor?"

"Oh... er... nothing much..." he began, but decided not to prevaricate, although he knew exactly what Peri's reaction would be. He took the bull by the horns and exclaimed,

"These!" producing from his pocket the largest stickiest chocolate bar Peri had ever seen. "All for the most unselfish of motives. Of course!" he grinned.

But Peri had not finished.

"Aside from your dodgy eating habits, Doctor, I am appalled that you, of all people should be so irresponsible! You should have done everything possible to help clear pollution on Earth – not cover up the fact that it hadn't been done. You really are appalling. I can't believe that you could let the people of Earth down so badly for the sake of a few chocolate bars. You have always professed to have a special fondness for them!" she added with disgust.

"What? Chocolate bars?" smirked the Doctor raising his eyebrows in innocent incomprehension.

"No! The people of Earth!" shouted Peri.

"Aaaah! I have my dear Peri. You don't quite understand, I'm afraid. In the eyes of the Vervalloochenen enforcement agency, it is the people of Earth that ARE the pollution! At least you now have another few thousand years in which to change your ways or risk attracting crop circles that are caused by the real thing rather than my humble efforts with a vacuum cleaner, a plank and piece of rope!"

He resisted the overwhelming temptation to pop a chocolate bar into her wide open mouth and, whistling jauntily, set the TARDIS rotors in motion.

A Wee Deoch an ... ?

Alistair Lethbridge-Stewart was irritated. He was an organised and methodical man by nature and disliked changing his well laid plans at the last minute, especially when such a change interfered with his only occasionally interesting private life. As a serving officer in His Majesty's forces, he was, of course, hard wired to obey the commands of superior officers at all times. However, things were quiet at the moment in terms of army activity and he had every reason to think that an interesting weekend lay ahead of him. The last few days had surprised him. He found himself looking forward to something in a way that he hadn't experienced before. He could easily become irritated when people asked him in all innocence if he was looking forward to something. That implied weakness and wasteful emotion to him and he liked to maintain a calm and business-like approach to his personal life as well as his life as an officer in Army.

The phone call from Leo Teynham, Billy Rutlidge's infuriatingly smug ADC, had prevented him from taking the sleeper up to Scotland as planned. He had been promised some fine shooting, excellent dining and, to Alistair even more persuasively, the opportunity to renew his acquaintance with Fiona Fraser, his intended host's fiery and fascinating sister. Alistair had known Nicol Fraser since they were at school together, where they had shared a dormitory, a love of sport and an aversion to Latin. He had the most vivid memories of his first meeting with his friend's younger sister, when Nicol's parents had brought her with them to watch an inter–school rugger match. Back then there was no hint of the beauty that would emerge from the chrysalis of her less than promising teenage years. She had been a gawky, freckled tomboy, who had gleefully heaped scorn on the boys' physical prowess, suggesting mischievously that she and her girlfriends could have done a much better job in the scrum than he and Nicol had managed. His reaction to her back then had been pretty typical for a thirteen year old boy. He had all but ignored her, apart from the automatic social niceties bred into his generation, until on a later occasion she had demonstrated that she was actually a 'good sort' by leaping into the air with unrestrained glee when her brother felled a hulking brute from the opposing team with a deft and crunching tackle. Aside from that one moment of grudging acceptance that she was 'not too bad for a girl,' he had forgotten about her until many years later when he had encountered her again at Nicol's engagement party in Argyllshire. This time no recognition of a fine rugby tackle was required to alert Alistair to his friend's sister's abundant charms. The gawky tomboy had metamorphosed into a slim, elegant bright-eyed young lady with the finest head of tumbling auburn hair that the young officer had ever set eyes upon. Being the gentleman that he was and by nature somewhat diffident, Alistair had left the party regretting that he had not had the courage to make his burgeoning interest in his friend's sister more evident than by courteously telling how lovely it was to see her again and enquiring after her health, before she was whisked off by a less timorous guest for the Gay Gordons. On subsequent occasions however, Alistair had seized the opportunity to spend time with this most beguiling of young ladies and had been gratified to note that his interest did not seem entirely one sided. He had therefore swiftly responded to the opportunity to further the course of his intended courtship of her and accepted the shooting party invitation in the certain knowledge not only that that she would be there but also that she had given him every encouragement to believe that she shared his enthusiasm in welcoming the opportunity to spend some more time together.

His eager anticipation of the incomparable thrill of beginning a new romantic adventure in the rugged splendour of Ardnamurchan peninsula, combined with some excellent shooting and all the lavish hospitality that went with it, had been rudely shattered therefore by Leo Teynham's phone call. Leo had been infuriatingly mysterious. He was a man who loved to demonstrate to others that he was privy to information that was denied to them. He did so by the simple expedient of hinting much but explaining little. He found that it was a technique that enhanced his image whilst infuriating others who were unable to voice their irritation because either his rank was superior to theirs or his position as ADC to the General gave him immunity from officers who outranked him. He curtly instructed Alistair that he should go immediately to Brighton, check into the Royal Albion Hotel and await contact from a Herr Hahnstier, who would brief him more fully about the purpose of the meeting..

Alistair began to protest,

"Look old chap, does it have to be me? Always happy to oblige old Billy the Kid, of course, but there's something frightfully important – of a – well – how shall I say? – of a personal nature – that, all things being equal, you know, I would really rather like to..."

He was cut off by the oleaginous Leo whose drawled response might perhaps have suggested insouciance to strangers. However, to Alistair it was clear that negotiation was not an option.

"Well, my dear fellow, I am, of course, in no position to judge whether this 'personal business' of yours is more important than our commanding officer's orders. Heaven only knows we all have private lives, Alistair – and we all know how personal commitments and our duty to our families and friends can rub up against our duty to our country – shall we say – 'inconveniently' from time to time. I suppose it is for each one of us to make that judgement call ourselves. But General Rutlidge was most insistent that it should be you. So... it's up to you, old chum."

He paused briefly.

"What would you like me to say to the old man? He did seem awfully keen that you were the only man for the job... but he didn't give me too many details about the nature of your rendezvous with Herr Whatsisname... er... Hanstier. Yes, that's it. Seemed to think the fewer people knew about this hush–hush business the better. But what he did tell me convinced me that it was pretty important to him...."

Alistair conceded defeat. He had no option but to bow to inevitability and obey his instructions without further demur. Until, in later life, he were to encounter that infuriating fellow, the Doctor, the possibility that instructions from a superior could be questionable, or indeed questioned (let alone ignored), simply never really occurred to him. He had taken the King's Commission and was an officer in his Majesty's Armed Forces. Had he been a stick of rock, then 'Duty' would have been the word that ran in bold letters through every fibre of his being. The image of Fiona's blue, blue eyes framed by the light dusting of freckles and topped by the fiery halo of her thick hair receded slowly from his vision and was replaced by Bradshaw's guide. He checked the train times to Brighton.

The journey down to the coast did not serve to lighten his mood. A travel warrant had been delivered to him by a uniformed motorcyclist, arriving mere minutes after he put the telephone down. Clearly his ability to drop everything at short notice had been taken for granted. The warrant, however, was not for first class travel, as he might have had reason to expect. Was this Teynham's far from subtle way of putting him in his place, he wondered? Or just a sign of the times? The train was crowded and seemed to be populated exclusively by the noisiest, most ill–disciplined children he had ever encountered and their seemingly oblivious parents. When he arrived in Brighton, the ticket collector had never seen an Army travel warrant before and whilst he could see that Alistair was wearing the uniform of an Army officer, he was a man who liked to exercise the authority that went along with the uniform that he himself wore. The stationmaster was summoned and immediately instructed his truculent subordinate in the niceties of the travel warrant and the appropriate way of dealing with them. He apologised profusely to the Brigadier, who by this time was only interested in getting to his hotel, where he fondly hoped there might be a bar that had a decent stock of single malt whisky. On leaving the station, he discovered that there were no taxis at the rank and every other passenger from his train, screaming brats included, was ahead of him in the queue.

Fortunately the walk to the Royal Albion Hotel was downhill. Unfortunately it was raining. He arrived at the reception desk fifteen minutes later, glum, moist and just a little bit tetchy.

He queued at the reception desk for several minutes while a corpulent gentleman complained about the fact that the noise of the sea had kept him awake the previous night, failing to accept this as the logical consequence of booking a room overlooking the promenade and, beyond that, the sea. Eventually he had the undivided attention of the receptionist. He was not one to trumpet his rank unnecessarily to civilians, so indicated that a room had been booked in the name of Lethbridge-Stewart.

"Let me see now sir, ah yes here we are – Grenadier Lethbridge-Stewart – yes that seems in order, sir."

"Er – Brigadier actually."

"Sorry sir?"

"Brigadier Lethbridge-Stewart. You said 'Grenadier.'"

"Oh sorry sir, that's what I have written here. Is there a difference, sir?"

"Yes... but it really doesn't matter. Can I have my key please?"

Alistair's day was not getting any better. All he wanted to do now was to have a quick dram and get this rendezvous out of the way.

The receptionist arched an eyebrow, pursed his lips and passed the key over to Alistair.

"Here you are," he paused for emphasis, "Brigadier!"

Alistair headed for the staircase aware of the jaded eyes of the receptionist boring into his back as he walked away.

Later that evening, after he had been sitting in the echoing, panelled lounge immediately adjacent to the reception foyer for over two hours, the porter brought him the message that a Mr. John Steer ("It was hard to get his name, sir – he spoke funny") had telephoned the hotel with a message for him. It transpired that Herr Hahnstier had been delayed in Berne and would not be arriving in Brighton until late Sunday evening. He apologised and hoped that Alistair would still be able to meet him. The same porter was then instantly entrusted with the task of bringing to Alistair the second large single malt that he had been resisting thitherto, in order to ensure that he could deal the more effectively with whatever surprises his expected intriguing appointment with the German might produce. However, a forty-eight hour delay in the meeting changed things considerably. He was irritated, not for the first time that day, but too good a soldier to do other than wait patiently for the arrival of the mysterious Herr Hahnstier. He looked out of the tall, lushly curtained windows over a choppy, grey sea that merged with a sky that was leaden with heavy and foreboding clouds. He found himself feeling extremely grateful that his family tradition and education had led him to an army career rather than a naval one. Not a night to be afloat, he thought, as he savoured his whisky, while ruefully contemplating this missed opportunity to spend time with the bonny wee lass that was even now dining with a score of other more eligible suitors in the distant Western Highlands.

Mel was irritated too. The Doctor had suddenly decided that his 991st birthday was not an anniversary that he could allow to pass without marking the occasion with some sort of appropriate celebration.

"And I know just the place!" he had exclaimed, striding purposefully towards the TARDIS console room. Mel knew the signs and was resigned to another bout of intergalactic travel agents' hyperbole about the Eye of Orion or the Ear of Hermes and was in the process of steeling herself to yet another thwarted attempt to show her the Universe's answer to the Grand Canyon, when he added "... and we'll leave the time and detailed location up to the old girl's serendipity circuits, I think. I love a mystery tour, don't you?"

He didn't wait to hear her response – and there was nothing new there. He busied himself with the controls of the TARDIS, chatting to it as he did so.

"When are you going to take me this time, eh old girl? Not before the industrial revolution, I think – but definitely not immediately after the Great Flood or the Ozone Wars... so restricted serendipity, I think, don't you?" He flicked a battery of switches and a lever or two, shut his eyes and flicked a couple more toggles and levers, and the familiar lurch, whine and visceral groaning sent them on their way.

So it was that Mel found herself in Brighton, following the Doctor through the corridors of the Royal Albion Hotel (in the dusty depth of whose wine cellars the TARDIS had materialised). Had she had a beard, not only would it have been a vivid red and bristling with frustration, but she would have been muttering darkly into it. It had simply not occurred to the Doctor that a former resident of Pease Pottage, Sussex, might not regard the attractions of Brighton with quite the same degree of unbridled enthusiasm as this overgrown Gallifreyan child seemed to be presently demonstrating to an uncaring world that was occupied at that moment mainly by her. But she forced herself to remember that it was his "birthday treat" so she should maybe restrain herself from protesting too much. Thinking of which......

"Doctor, what is so special about your 991st birthday, anyway?"

"What do you mean?"

"Well", she replied patiently, "a hundredth birthday, or five hundredth – even nine hundredth – they would be worthy of celebration – and with your thousandth coming up so soon, why waste such a wonderful experience as a visit to Brighton..." and she quickly continued as he drew an indignant breath to query her heavily sarcastic tone "... on a 991st birthday?"

He looked at her with what seemed to be genuine rather than feigned perplexity and was about to ask her, in turn, what was so special about a one thousandth birthday, compared with the numerical purity of a prime numbered one, especially a circular prime number that remains prime on any cyclic rotation of its digits. Wasn't she a computer programmer after all? But before he got to express his surprise at her numerical naïveté, he was obliged to swerve to the left slightly to avoid the head waiter, who had planted himself in front of this bizarrely dressed stranger to enquire if he was the children's entertainer booked for Lord Roxburgh's daughter's 7th birthday party. Lord Roxburgh had been most insistent that his spoilt brat of a daughter should have the 'best birthday ever' as the alternative would be that Lady Roxburgh would never let him hear the end of it. And if he, a peer of the realm, was to be inconvenienced in this way, he would make sure that the Royal Albion Hotel and all who worked in it would regret it. The head waiter was therefore in the direct line of fire if the children's entertainer was late or incompetent. And he was already the former!

Before the stressed hotel employee could open his mouth, the Doctor's sudden lurch to the left resulted in his collision with a hapless waitress who was passing behind him. This caused her to deposit a plate of cream cakes into the lap of a rather pleasant looking young lady sitting at an adjacent table.

As the head waiter pursued the waitress, who had fled the scene in floods of tears, to get her back to help clear up the result of her clumsiness, the Doctor swept onwards, oblivious both to the unfortunate result of his erratic progress and the presence a few feet away of an old friend. The latter, despite having witnessed the whole incident, had no idea of course that its instigator was to figure so largely in his future life, albeit in radically different corporeal forms.

The Doctor marched out into the grey mist of the evening and took a deep breath.

"Ah the ozone, Mel. That wonderful salty tang in the air! That enchantingly haunting crepuscular light beckoning to us across the ebbing tide like lighthouse of Pharos in ancient Alexandria! Come on, I'll race you across the shingle!" And he bounded off again with an enthusiasm that might have been infectious had it not reminded Mel of countless days spent here with her parents when she was a child. Resignedly she followed the birthday boy into the gloom.

Back inside the hotel in the absence of any help from the hotel staff and true to his background and nature, Alistair stood up and went to the aid of the damsel in distress, who was ineffectually trying to deal unaided with the effects of a tray of cream cakes landing in her lap.

He found himself looking into a pair of twinkling brown eyes, set in an open, friendly face and said,

"Alistair Lethbridge-Stewart. May I be of assistance, Miss ...er..?"

"My name," she replied," is Doris. And as to whether you can be of assistance to me... well, unless you happen to own a laundry or have a hidden supply of dresses in my size, I'm at a loss to know how to respond to your most gallant offer." She glanced down at her lap and added mischievously, "Would you care for a meringue, Alistair Lethbridge-Stewart?"

She giggled infectiously and Alistair found himself reflecting that the next forty–eight hours might not be quite so dull after all, as thoughts of his missed weekend in the Glens receded from his mind.

And not only did those thoughts recede at that moment but they did not, he was later to recall, ever surface again.

Meanwhile leaning into the wind and spray and trying to protect herself from their effects on her hair and clothing, Mel was gazing balefully at the Doctor, as the words "bracing" and "invigorating" floated back over his shoulder in her direction. She also heard him giving what seemed to her to be unnecessary emphasis to the words "*prime* of my life", but their significance was lost on her.

Also by Colin Baker
from www.hirstbooks.com

Also by Colin Baker
from www.hirstbooks.com

The Author and Publisher would like to thank the following people:

Brian Adams	Paul Engelberg
Janet Adkins	Michael Evans
Darren Allen	Stewart Fearon
Kade Allen	Ross Fletcher
Tony Amis	Michael Flett
Julie Augustin	Alex Frazer-Harrison
Mark Bailey	Cynthia Garland
Richard Black	Kev Garnsworthy
Stephanie Black	Hannah Garvey
Nicholas Blake	Peter Gilham
Philip Brennan	Ian Greenfield
Andrew Brook	Aaron Gregson
Jason Brooks	Dan Hall
Laura Brotherton	Andrew Harrison
Nicholas Caluda	Ben Haughton
Stephen Candy	Julie Hayes
Darren Chandler	Rebekah Helvie
Roger Clark	Steve Herbert
Joel Cleasby	Edward Hipkiss
Mike Cook	Martin Holmes
Brian Cook	Steve Horsley
Joe Cooper	Daniel Humes
Catherine Cranston	Mark Humphrey
Lauren Crawford	Linda Isele
Manu Das	David Jacovelli
Alex Day	Blayne Jensen
Steven Dieter	David Johnson
Trevor Donnelly	Simon Kemp
Mark Ducker	Christopher Kerr
Cory Eadson	Derek Kettlety
Barnaby Eaton-Jones	Michael Kincaid
Gemma Edwards	Andrew Kitching

Gary Knowles
Chad Knueppe
Robert Konjek
David Larkin
Michael Leader
Christopher Leather
Tristan Maddocks
Adrian Maj
Steven Matthewman
Ben Mcclory
James C Mcfetridge
Ian Mclachlan
Alan Mcwhan
W A Messingham
Stuart Mitchell
Grant Mitchell
Karl Morton IV
Paul Norman
Dave Owen
Marcus Palmer
Matthew Partis
Stephen Pasqua
Alister Pearson
John Pettigrew
Mark Phippen
Paul Pickford
Shanti Roy
Iain Rylands
Paul Salvi
Blake Samples
Tina Seager
Alexandra Shewan
Oliver Sibley
Bryan Simcott
Tim Small
Marianne Smeathers

Douglas Smith
Johnathan Smith
Sean-Paul Smith
Karen Smith
J.R. Southall
Brian Steed
Andrew Stingel
Samantha Stone
Rachel Taylor
Casey Thomas
Jan Thomson
Robert Turner
Richard Unwin
Martin Wakefield
Janet Wakeling
Stephen James Walker
David Wallington
Ian Wheeler
Ruth Wheeler
Martin Wiggins
Robert Williams
Raina Williams
Alex Wilson-Fletcher
Susan Wilt
Stephanie Wolfe
David Wright
Anthony Zehetner
Brian Zitzelberger

More books for Doctor Who fans, from www.hirstpublishing.com

www.hirstpublishing.com

www.colinbakeronline.com

www.facebook.com/hirstbooks

Hirst Publishing on Twitter: @hirstbooks

Colin Baker on Twitter: @SawbonesHex

Meet the stars of TV & Film

Our Celebrity Signings bring you the stars of
Doctor Who, Torchwood, James Bond, Hammer Horror, Red Dwarf, Blake's 7
& much more.

Our shows and events take place all over the country

For more information on our next signings & shows visit
www.tenthplanetevents.co.uk
1000s of celebrity autographs also available from our online store

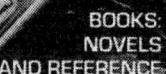